FOREVER LOVE AT WILDFLOWER LOCK

HANNAH LYNN

Boldwood

First published in Great Britain in 2025 by Boldwood Books Ltd.

Copyright © Hannah Lynn, 2025

Cover Design by Alexandra Allden

Cover Images: Shutterstock

Every effort has been made to obtain the necessary permissions with reference to copyright material, both illustrative and quoted. We apologise for any omissions in this respect and will be pleased to make the appropriate acknowledgements in any future edition.

A CIP catalogue record for this book is available from the British Library.

Paperback ISBN 978-1-83603-781-1

Large Print ISBN 978-1-83603-782-8

Hardback ISBN 978-1-83603-780-4

Ebook ISBN 978-1-83603-783-5

Kindle ISBN 978-1-83603-784-2

Audio CD ISBN 978-1-83603-775-0

MP3 CD ISBN 978-1-83603-776-7

Digital audio download ISBN 978-1-83603-779-8

This book is printed on certified sustainable paper. Boldwood Books is dedicated to putting sustainability at the heart of our business. For more information please visit https://www.boldwoodbooks.com/about-us/sustainability/

Boldwood Books Ltd, 23 Bowerdean Street, London, SW6 3TN

www.boldwoodbooks.com

ALSO BY HANNAH LYNN

The Holly Berry Sweet Shop Series

The Sweet Shop of Second Chances

Love Blooms at the Second Chances Sweet Shop

High Hopes at the Second Chances Sweet Shop

Family Ties at the Second Chances Sweet Shop

Sunny Days at the Second Chances Sweet Shop

A Summer Wedding at the Second Chances Sweet Shop

Snowflakes Over the Second Chances Sweet Shop

The Wildflower Lock Series

New Beginnings at Wildflower Lock

Coffee and Cake at Wildflower Lock

Blue Skies Over Wildflower Lock

Forever Love at Wildflower Lock

Standalone Novels

In at the Deep End

The Side Hustle

Hannah Lynn writing as H.M Lynn

The Head Teacher

To Ruth Knight and Beverley Mulley for all their support.

1

Sometimes, when Daisy May looked back on the last two years, it was easy to believe that she had packed more into those twenty-four months than the entire previous twenty-five years of her life. And it was all down to the *September Rose:* the wide beam canal boat she had inherited from her father.

To start with, she probably wouldn't have got back into painting, had she not found her late father's art supplies in the boat. She certainly wouldn't have set up her own business – a coffee shop on the canal. She wouldn't have met her boyfriend, and love of her life, Theo, and she most definitely wouldn't have travelled across the country in a canal boat to see him.

There were other things, which weren't so ideal. She wouldn't have had to deal with a temporary, but still major, fallout with her mother. She wouldn't have known what it was like to have your windows smashed in by a tree in the middle of the night, or be broken into by someone she believed was a friend. But however significant these incidents had felt at the time, they were all minor compared to what she had gained. Particularly now Theo had moved back to Wildflower Lock.

The twelve-month separation had been hard. As much as they had hoped they would be able to spend their spare time together, spare time wasn't something either of them had much of. And so, when a job appeared on the waterways near Chelmsford, Theo had been quick to apply. Their hopes were answered when he had been offered the placement after a single telephone interview and now he had been back on Wildflower Lock for sixth months.

Things weren't quite as convenient as they had been. The *Narrow Escape* – Theo's boat – was no longer moored up next to Daisy's, but on the other side of the canal, where the *Ariadne* had been. Giving up the *Ariadne* had been a difficult decision for Yvonne. She had lived on Wildflower Lock for decades and had a lifetime full of memories wrapped up with the water. But after a health scare during her trip across country with Daisy, she had decided to find somewhere a little more stable to live. So she had sold up and moved to Woodham Mortimer a few miles away. She still came down to the lock several times a week though, to see Daisy and Theo, not to mention Johnny.

'Where is Theo?' Daisy said, as she reached down and rubbed the dog's head. Just like Theo and Wildflower Lock, Daisy could no longer imagine her life without Johnny in it. Although he was meant to be Theo's dog, and went out to work with him every day, the moment Theo arrived back at the canal, Johnny would bound out of the van and run straight to the *September Rose* – or to wherever Daisy was. At night-time, they tended to sleep on the *Narrow Escape*, with Johnny at the foot of the bed, and on the weekends when Theo would help Daisy run the coffee shop, Johnny would sit on the hull, wagging his tail at the customers until Daisy or Theo could take him for a walk or at least offer him a quick belly rub. Life was as close to perfect as Daisy could ever remember. But that night, it felt like something strange was going on.

It was a Friday afternoon, and the weather was stunning, so Daisy had kept the coffee shop open a little later than normal. As such, it was gone six before she finally closed the shutters and called it a day. Normally, when the weather was this great and Theo knew Daisy would be busy, he opted to work late too so he could use the accumulated hours to spend more time with her when the weather wasn't so great. Normally, he wouldn't come in until after seven, but Daisy was just bringing in the chalkboard from outside when Johnny appeared and Theo was hot on his heals.

'You're on your own?' Theo said. He looked surprisingly confused as he spoke, although why Daisy wasn't exactly sure. It was true, the girls did come down and spend a lot of time at the canal, particularly now there was an empty boat to sleep in most nights, but Daisy always told Theo when they were planning on coming and this weekend it was Saturday and Sunday that they had arranged to visit.

'Just you and me tonight,' Daisy responded with a grin.

'Right. Yes.' Theo didn't look as pleased by this remark as Daisy had expected him to. Instead, a slight pout appeared on his lips before he spoke again. 'Are you okay to go over to mine and look after Johnny for a couple of hours tonight?'

'Okay? Where are you going?' Daisy said. 'I thought you wanted to watch that new Julia Roberts film tonight?'

Theo glanced down the towpath. A slight sheen of sweat coated his brow.

'Yes, I know… It's only, something's come up at work.'

'And you don't want to take Johnny with you?'

The pair normally spent every working hour together and every person who worked or lived on the canals knew Johnny by name. Daisy even suspected that several people came to the coffee shop just to see him. Although she didn't complain. Customers were customers.

'It's a... a swan situation...' Theo said, glancing down at his watch.

'A swan situation?'

'I don't want Johnny to be there with them.'

Daisy crinkled her nose. Johnny wasn't normally an issue around swans or ducks or any animals that he had encountered at Wildflower Lock, but clearly this situation was serious. Daisy couldn't quite remember the last time she had seen Theo looking this flustered.

'Okay, well, sure. I'll just lock up and go over now.'

'I can lock up,' Theo said. 'I've got keys.'

'I thought you needed to go?'

'I do... but it's... You're right. You lock up. I'll go.'

Still feeling confused by the whole situation, Daisy headed inside to grab her keys and phone. Despite his apparent need to leave, Theo followed her onto the stern and waited there until she reappeared.

'Any idea how long you're going to be?' Daisy asked as she locked the door.

Theo shook his head. 'I don't think I'll be back until it's dark.'

'Really?' Daisy said. The summer months meant it didn't get dark until nearly ten. She couldn't imagine what kind of swan situation would require over three hours to sort out, but maybe that was why Theo was the person who worked on the canals and not her.

'Okay, well, we'll just be at yours when you get back.'

Theo nodded, though it didn't look like he was listening to her at all. Instead, he was staring at his phone.

'Right, I guess I'll see you later,' Theo said as they stood on the towpath, although considering what a hurry he was supposed to be in, he wasn't actually moving. Instead, he was staring at Daisy as if he were expecting her to move. And she was going to, but only across the canal to the *Narrow Escape*. It didn't really seem like that far to go.

'Can I have a kiss?' Daisy said, given how that was the way they always parted.

'Of course. Of course.' It felt like it was the first time all afternoon that Theo was paying Daisy any attention, although his lips had barely touched hers, when he suddenly jerked away.

'Oh, what a surprise,' he said, a wide grin on his face. 'Look who's here.'

Daisy was one of those people who had had the same best friends since school. Yes, she had met other people, made other friends too, but none had ever compared to Bex and Claire. No matter what the occasion, whether it was an hour of need, or a celebration, Daisy could always guarantee they would be the first ones there with wine or tissues or sometimes both. Normally Claire's daughter, Amelia, would be in tow too. Though she was still too young to work, she leapt at every opportunity to come to Wildflower Lock. Once there, she would spend the time drawing or throwing rocks for Johnny – his favourite game – while absorbing everything she could about the business, ready for when she was finally old enough to help. Though while Amelia couldn't work the coffee machine, Claire and Bex would sometimes take time out from London life, just to help Daisy out. They had even dog-sat Johnny when she and Theo had gone for a weekend trip to Edinburgh. She spoke to one, if not both of them on the phone almost every single day and knew what their plans were from summer holidays to Christmas lunch, even though it was over half a year away. Which was why seeing them there caught her so much by surprise.

'I didn't know you were coming down,' Daisy said, breaking away from Theo to hug her friends. 'What are you doing? I thought you were coming down tomorrow.'

'We were. We are,' Bex answered. 'But the weather's really good—'

'And she was complaining about being in the city—' Claire cut over her friend.

'And so we decided to come down here. See if you wanted to take Johnny for a walk to the pub.'

'And not a moment too soon,' Theo muttered.

Daisy turned to face him, not quite sure she had caught what he said properly.

'What was that?' she said.

'I just meant that it's about time Johnny had a proper walk, that was all,' Theo replied. His gaze skirted past Daisy, and he looked at the girls instead. 'We've had quite a lot of time in the van today,' he said. 'Quite a lot of driving. He'll need a long walk. A very long walk.'

Daisy was about to ask where they'd gone and why Johnny had had to be in the van so much. Even when Theo did consultancy work – which would sometimes see him spending nights away – he always made sure that walking Johnny was a priority. No wonder he was looking stressed if he hadn't managed that.

'In that case, we should probably get going now,' Claire said, at which point Theo nodded enthusiastically.

'Yes, yes. Absolutely. You guys should go get Johnny and I should get to the shops.'

'To the shops? I thought you were dealing with swans for work?' Daisy said in confusion.

'Yes, yes, I am. Only I've got to go to the hardware store. Before I get to the swans, we need some rope.'

Daisy raised her eyebrows. It made more sense why Theo didn't want to take Johnny with him on this escapade, but he probably should have gone to the store to fetch the rope before-hand. After all, she wasn't even sure it was still open.

'Well, you guys go for a nice walk, have a nice drink. Take your time, but don't drink too much?' Theo said.

'Sure,' Daisy replied, not sure why everything felt so abrupt and odd about the conversation. Yet before she could even check if Theo was okay, or kiss him goodbye, he was already sprinting towards the car park.

'Did Theo seem strange to you?' Daisy said to the girls as they crossed over the gate towards the *Narrow Escape*.

'I don't think so,' Claire replied. 'He sounded perfectly normal to me.'

'Did he really?' Daisy wasn't convinced. 'I don't know. Maybe he's stressed. You know, it's not like he gets a day off ever. If he's not working on the canals, he's working in the coffee shop. I try to tell him he doesn't need to, but he always insists. Maybe he should book a weekend away so he won't feel guilty for not working.'

'I'm sure it's just because it's Friday,' Bex said, joining in the conversation. 'He's fine. So, do you want to have a shower or something? I'll have a quick search for nice restaurants in the area and book a table. I don't mind not drinking, so I'll drive.'

'Drive to a restaurant?' Daisy shook her head. 'I need to look after Johnny, remember? He's been cooped up too much today. And I thought you wanted to go for a walk too. We were gonna head to the pub. We spoke about this two minutes ago.'

Bex shook her head and rolled her eyes.

'Gosh, sorry, crazy day. Can't get my thoughts straight. It's probably this heat.'

Daisy wasn't going to deny it was hot, but it wasn't like Bex not to pay attention to things and having both her and Theo acting oddly didn't make Daisy feel great, but thankfully Claire was still her normal, practical self.

'I had a quick look on the map,' Claire said. 'And there's a lovely pub in Danbury. We could go there.'

'Danbury?' Holly winced a little. 'That's over an hour's walk away.'

'I know. Didn't Theo say Johnny needed to properly stretch his legs?'

'I know, but then that's an hour there, an hour or so having a drink and something to eat, and another hour to walk back. We won't be home until gone nine.' Daisy struggled to believe that after a long week at work, the last thing her friends wanted to do was spend two hours walking. She waited for Bex to object to Claire's suggestion, but instead, she grinned.

'Perfect, so we're back by ten,' Bex said. 'Will it be dark by then?' she added, throwing a look at Claire with an expression Daisy couldn't quite read.

'Hold on a second, I'll check,' Claire replied before tapping away at her phone. 'Yes, yes, it will be. It should start getting dark when we're walking back.'

'See, that sounds dangerous,' Daisy said. 'We could go somewhere a bit closer and not have to come back in the dark. Or we could take Johnny for a walk for an hour or so, then come back to Theo's. We've got a few bottles of wine in.'

'No, we don't want to stay here,' Bex said with an unusual amount of fervour. 'This'll be an adventure.'

Daisy let out a low internal groan. As much as she fancied curling up in the *Narrow Escape*, Johnny needed a proper walk, and she knew she wasn't going to get out of this one.

'Fine,' she said with a sigh, 'but I'm getting my torch for the way back. The last thing I want is to walk home in the dark.'

While the walk from Wildflower Lock to Danbury wasn't a quick one, it followed a reasonably straightforward footpath along the edges of various fields.

'I can't believe this is what you guys want to be doing,' Daisy said as Johnny ran ahead of them. Bex really wasn't dressed for a long walk, given that she had come straight from the office and was wearing white linen trousers and wedge sandals that didn't look easy to walk in, though she didn't complain.

'Are you kidding?' Claire said. 'I love it. I don't know why we've not done this walk before. I'll do it with Amelia next time we come down.'

'Speaking of Amelia, is she still coming tomorrow?'

'I guess we'll just have to wait and see,' Claire said, throwing a glance at Bex.

'Wait and see what?' Daisy said. 'What's going on with the pair of you? You've been acting weird since you got here.'

'We have not,' Bex said, stressing her words far more than seemed natural.

'We are just in a good mood,' Claire seconded. 'Enjoying the sunshine. That's all. So how are things? How's your mum? Did she patch things up with Nicholas?'

Daisy's mother, Pippa, always had a sketchy love life, frequently picking the wrong type of men. And Daisy had been less than pleased when she had ignited a relationship with the grumpy Nicholas, a fellow canal boat dweller on Wildflower Lock. But despite Daisy's initial reservations, she had grown fond of Nicholas and had been unexpectedly saddened when they had broken up a few months earlier. This sadness had been compounded by the fact that Daisy had to deal with all her mother's melancholy, which often involved drinking a bottle of wine or more in the *September Rose* while lamenting about all her failed relationships. Fortunately, they seemed to have patched things up recently.

'They got back together about a month ago,' Daisy told Claire. 'He was pushing Mum to retire early. That was the issue. Or find a job closer. She doesn't want to stop working, she's not sure she can afford to, but I think she's considered looking for something closer. They seem to be happy enough now. I'm sure I told you this all on the phone the other day, though.'

'You're right,' Claire said, 'you did. Sorry. I think the pre-summer holiday panic has set in. I'm not sure how I'm going to cope with the full six weeks. Honestly, you would not believe the number of clubs Amelia wants me to take her to. Gymnastics, art, drama camp, football camp. I might as well become a taxi service. But I suppose it happens to all of us, right?'

Daisy shrugged as she watched Johnny running ahead on the path in front of her.

'I mean, I guess so,' she said. 'Maybe not. I don't know if I can see it happening to me.'

'What about you and Theo? Haven't you talked about having children?' Bex asked, throwing yet another gaze in Claire's direction. It was almost as if they were refusing to acknowledge Daisy was even there.

'No, not really.'

'You haven't? Isn't that weird?' Claire said.

Daisy shrugged again, not sure why her shoulders were starting to tighten. 'I don't know, I guess not. We're happy the way things are at the minute.'

'I know, but—'

'I guess it'll come up when it comes up,' Daisy said. She was about to change the subject away from her and Theo to the far more interesting topic of Bex's love life when Johnny let out a loud bark. There, ahead of them, the village had just come into view and right on the edge of it, was the pub.

'Thank goodness for that,' she said, excited to sit down for the first time all day. 'I'm starving.'

As was normally the case when the girls went out for dinner, they got a bottle of wine to share between the three of them. Although when they finished it, they seemed less than keen to get another.

'We've got to walk all the way across the fields back to Wild-flower Lock and these wedges have pretty high heels,' Bex said, as if this was a new piece of news to them.

'Actually, yes, we should probably start heading back now, shouldn't we?' Claire looked at her watch. 'It should be dark by the time we get back.'

Daisy was struggling to understand her friends' obsession with darkness, but she wanted to go back too. Fingers crossed Theo would be home soon.

'I take it from the fact you've both been drinking that you're crashing at mine tonight?' Daisy said.

'I think that's the plan,' Bex replied, looking over at Claire, who nodded.

'Yeah, we'll stay at yours, whatever happens.'

There was something about the way the girls were wording themselves that Daisy just couldn't make sense of. Even more puzzling was how they had been shooting glances across the table at one another all through the meal. Then again, it was only a month or so until her birthday, Daisy reasoned, so maybe they were planning something for that.

'Come on then,' Bex said, standing up and picking up Johnny's lead from where it had been wrapped around the leg of the table. 'We should get going.'

If Daisy had thought her friends' attitudes during the meal had been peculiar, it was nothing compared to their behaviour on the walk back. To start with, the conversation had been based on Johnny and dogs. If Daisy was planning on getting another dog, or breeding from Johnny. What type of dog Amelia wanted and why Claire just couldn't see it working. All the different dogs that men Bex had dated had owned. That type of thing, but the closer they got to Wildflower Lock, the stranger it became. Every time Claire went to speak, Bex would cut over her and say the opposite.

When Claire said, 'I think we should speed up. We've been gone for quite a while,' Bex immediately countered her.

'I don't think we need to speed up at all. I think it's a good idea to walk slowly. Besides, I'm wearing heels. It's easier to go slow.'

'But maybe if you go a bit faster, you never know what might be waiting for you.'

'Maybe nothing, if I go too fast.'

'What are you two on about?' Daisy said, utterly confused.

Immediately, the conversation flicked back to dog breeds, where it stayed for a little while longer.

'How far are we from Wildflower Lock now?' Bex asked just a few minutes later. 'Ten minutes? Does that sound right?'

Daisy crinkled up her nose. 'No, I'd say it's another half an hour. You wanted to walk slowly, remember.'

'You're right, perhaps we should speed up.'

With the speed now a far brisker walk, the girls' conversation continued, this time around a topic that Daisy had next to no experience in.

'I think this time of year would be perfect to get married, don't you? You're guaranteed sun this time of year.'

'Not always.' Bex was there with her counter again. 'A colleague of mine got married mid-August and their marquee totally flooded. But I guess it depends on where you would do it.'

'What about you, Daisy?' Claire said.

Daisy was currently looking at Johnny running ahead. He was generally a very good dog, and she had never seen him so much as bark aggressively at another, but the last thing she wanted was for a rabbit to appear in the field and for him to dart after it.

'Daisy?'

Daisy turned back to the girls and found them looking at her with peculiarly locked stares.

'Sorry, what did you say?' Daisy asked, with Johnny now walking back to her.

'We were talking about weddings. This time of year? What do you think?'

'Oh, I don't know. I've not really been to that many.'

Her previous life of moving from one job to another meant Daisy hadn't really had time to form close enough relationships with work colleagues to be invited to weddings. And as for her home friends, there was only really Bex and Claire. Claire's wedding now felt like it was decades ago, and as for Bex, Daisy couldn't imagine her settling down any time soon.

'You know, I was thinking about that wedding I went to the other year where they had owls bring the rings down the aisle. It was awesome. Is that something you'd do, Daisy?' Bex said.

'Me?' Daisy replied.

'Yes, or maybe you could use Johnny as a ring bearer.'

'That's a great idea,' Claire said, clasping her hands in delight. 'He'd look so cute with one of those little doggy bow ties on.'

'Really, I think you might be getting a little carried away with things here. Theo and I have only been together two years, remember.'

'I know, but you know, right? That's what people say, isn't it? When you know, you know.'

Daisy pondered the question, although she didn't have to think about it for that long. Of course she knew. She had known before they had been together. When she had done everything she could to deny how much she felt for him, because the truth was it was terrifying to love someone that deeply. Because as soon as you did, it gave them the ability to hurt you. And while she didn't think that Theo would hurt her right now, she'd never thought that about her ex either. The one thing her previous relationship had taught her was to expect the unexpected. You could never take anything for granted.

Bex and Claire were already talking about something else, but even though the conversation had moved on, the thoughts continued to mull around in the back of Daisy's head, and as she pushed open the gate that led into Wildflower Lock, she couldn't help but raise it again.

'Do people really still believe in The One?' she said. 'In actual soulmates? It's a pretty big statement to make, right, that with all the people in the world, you just happen to find the only one who is meant for you.'

'I'm still looking for him,' Bex said.

'And I think that Ian and I are forever,' Claire added. 'I thought he was my soulmate at fifteen and I think that now too. There's no one in the world I could ever imagine loving the way I do him. Or having as much fun with.'

'I'm not saying I don't love Theo,' Daisy said, worried that they were misinterpreting what she was saying. 'Of course I do. More than anyone. I'm just not sure I'm ready to commit to the idea of The One, that's all.'

Behind her, Bex cleared her throat.

'Any chance you might be willing to commit sometime soon?' she said.

'What?' Daisy replied. 'What do you mean?'

She looked at her friend, waiting for an answer, but Bex didn't reply. Instead, her lips were pressed tightly together, and when Daisy moved her attention to Claire, she noticed tears were filling her friend's eyes.

'What is going on?' Daisy said. 'Why are you guys being so odd? This isn't just because I said I don't believe in soulmates, is it? You've been acting strange all day. Why did you come down today?'

Rather than replying, Bex simply nodded her head down past Daisy towards where the *September Rose* was moored.

'What? What aren't you telling me?' Daisy said turning around. That was when she saw it. As the breath flew from her lungs, she lifted her hand to cover her mouth.

'Oh my God,' she said.

6

Daisy stepped toward the girls, her hand still covering her face. She wasn't entirely sure what she was seeing. At least, she wasn't sure she believed what she was seeing. And with each footstep, she didn't know whether to stop or speed up.

A boat, in the location of the *September Rose*'s mooring, was lit up, but she couldn't understand how or why. But as she drew a little closer, there was no doubt to what she was seeing.

The *September Rose* had been covered in lights. Fairy lights. They were wound around the windows and the hatch. Wrapped around the bow, and placed in rows across the roof, turning it into a canopy of lights. Thousands and thousands of bright white lights gleaming out into the night. As Daisy got closer, she spotted several candles balanced on the bow. Her pulse rocketed and her heart leapt in her chest. For a moment, she almost broke out into a sprint until a second later when she realised they were fake. No one in their right mind would put real candles on a wooden boat. Still, her pulse didn't lower entirely. Why did the *September Rose* look like that and who the hell had done it? Theo was working late – he had a swan emergency to deal with. Only why would he be dealing with a swan emergency at this time of night? Even if it was on a canal, surely someone would have just rung Animal Rescue? That was when it all clicked into place.

Theo's peculiar behaviour when he had come home, all the conversations on the walk back about when it was going to be dark and the girls ensuring she was away from the canal for a decent length of time. It was nothing to do with taking Johnny for a walk at all.

Daisy's heart hammered in her chest as she approached the *September Rose*. It didn't feel real. None of it felt real. She swallowed back the lump that had risen in her throat and tried to steady her breathing. This couldn't possibly be what she thought it was, could it? As she drew up next to the bow, her heart was all the way up in her mouth, and her knees had started trembling, too. Was she supposed to go in? It was her boat, her home, but at that moment, she didn't know if she was meant to wait outside or if she even wanted to go in. It was all just too overwhelming.

For a split second, Daisy closed her eyes and took a deep breath in. Then, deciding she was going to ask the girls what they thought she should do, she opened her eyes again, only for the front door of the boat to open.

'Theo?' Daisy said, as he appeared on the bow. Wordlessly, he stepped onto the towpath. As normally happened when they had been separated for any length of time, Johnny rushed over to greet him, but Daisy stayed exactly where she was. Her eyes locked on Theo. Although at that moment, he didn't look like her Theo. A deep frown creased his forehead and his hands were clenched at his sides, as if he was trying to stop them from trembling.

'Theo...'

'I wasn't sure...'

They started speaking simultaneously, then cut off at the exact same time, too. Daisy felt her cheeks flush with colour.

'Is it too much?' Theo said, speaking again before Daisy had a chance to think. 'It seemed like a good idea, but then I started and couldn't stop and it's too much, isn't it? It's too much.'

'It's not too much,' Daisy said, glancing over at the boat and the thousands of lights that were twinkling. 'Okay, maybe you could have gone a little less crazy with the lights. I can't imagine what my electricity bill is going to be after this.'

Theo looked devastated.

'I knew it. It was a ridiculous idea.'

Daisy hastened towards him. 'No, I'm joking. I was joking. It's perfect. It's absolutely perfect. I... I don't need this, I didn't need this.'

Daisy had never thought about what it would be like when Theo proposed. She had assumed that they might make that type of commitment at some point in the future, but they had been so content as they were, it hadn't crossed her mind that much. But of course, she should have known that if the day ever arrived, he would go out on a limb to make sure everything was as incredible as possible. If, of course, this was a proposal, she reasoned to herself. He still hadn't actually said the words yet. Maybe she had got the wrong end of the stick.

Just as she had the thought, Theo reached out, took her hands and lowered himself onto one knee.

'Daisy May, you have turned my world upside down.' A smile flitted across his lips, and Daisy felt her heart swell in anticipation. It was going to happen. It was actually going to happen. Theo was going to propose to her. She bit down on her lip and waited for him to ask the question.

'You are the most amazing woman I have ever met. You are talented, funny, kind, generous, so damn hard-working. Every morning I wake up, and I don't understand how I got so lucky to be with you.'

Sniffing back the lump in her throat, Daisy felt a trickle down her cheek and wiped it away. She wasn't sure when she had started crying, but she was.

'Daisy, there is nothing I want more than to wake up every morning of my life with you.'

7

Daisy was staring at Theo, or rather, she was staring at the ring he was holding in his hand. It was absolutely perfect. A large central diamond haloed by a ring of small sapphires and rubies, and highlighted by a sparkling gold band. By the looks of things, it was an antique. A one-off. Totally unique. Just like the pair of them and their relationship.

'Not that I'm worried or anything, but you are making me a little nervous,' Theo said, still looking up at her. 'A reply would be good at some point. It's surprisingly painful, kneeling like this too.'

'Oh, yes, of course, yes,' Daisy said, brushing her hands against her cheeks, surprised to find they were still wet with tears. 'Of course, it's a yes.'

With a smile broader than she would have ever thought possible, Theo stood up and slipped the ring onto her finger. It was a perfect fit and even more impressive close up, with the way the rubies and sapphires tapered and the intricate filigree of the band. Daisy was still trying to take in all the details when a small chorus of cheers erupted behind her.

'Woohoo!'

Daisy didn't give herself time to think. Instead, she turned and raced towards her friends as they ran towards her and the group collided with such force into a hug, she almost toppled over. But it was worth it, just to see their insane grins up close.

'Wow,' Claire said. 'You had us worried for a minute there.'

'What are you on about? I wasn't worried for one second,' Bex said. 'Now, where is the Champagne? It's time to crack it open.'

'Hold on a second, I want to get a proper look at that ring first,' Claire said, pulling Daisy's hand towards her. 'Oh my God, that is stunning. Wow.'

'It is, isn't it?' Daisy said, lifting her hand up and turning her wrist slightly so that the light hit all the gemstones. Theo approached the group and wrapped his arms around her waist.

'Happy?' he asked.

'Very,' Daisy replied.

It was as she stood there, with her eyes locked on Theo's, that she realised she hadn't kissed him since accepting his proposal. She had been too overwhelmed with the ring and the girls. It was a mistake she quickly rectified. With her left hand pressed up against his cheek, she planted her lips against his. It was the most perfect kiss. Her first kiss as an engaged woman. And it could have gone on forever, had it not been for the voice that spoke behind her.

'Girls, I wasn't expecting to see you today? Is something going on?'

The voice called Daisy to break away from the kiss with a jerk. She was torn. She wanted the moment to go on for as long as possible, but at the same time, she wanted to tell everyone her news. And top of that list, as the girls already knew, was her mother, who she knew at that moment was standing right behind her.

'Does she know?' she whispered to Theo.

'No. I thought you'd want to be the one to tell her.'

'Thank you,' she said, then offered him one more quick kiss on the lips before turning back around and holding out her hand towards her mum.

'Theo asked me to marry him, and I said yes!'

8

It was a party. Daisy's mother had sent Nicholas straight back to the *Jeanette* to fetch several more bottles of Champagne and while there were fewer fairy lights inside the *September Rose* than outside, it had still been transformed, as much by the people as by the decoration. All the squeals and laughter – combined with the decorated boat – had attracted the attention of several other Wildflower Lock residents, and there were currently over twenty people crammed into the canal boat, all congratulating Theo and Daisy. There were also several out on the towpath with their drinks, and offering the various towpath dogs – including Johnny – plenty of attention.

'So, all this was planned, the girls coming down to take me out for a long walk. All the delays to make sure I didn't come back too soon. They were in on this?'

'You can't blame me for needing a bit of help, can you?' Theo said. His hand had stayed firmly around Daisy's waist the whole time, and she had no intention of changing it. Being close to Theo was definitely her favourite place to be.

'But how long have they known for? You didn't just plan this in a day, I assume.'

'They may have known my intentions for a little while,' Theo replied, before kissing Daisy lightly on her lips.

'I can't believe they kept it a secret from me, if I'm honest.'

'No, neither can I. Although Claire decided not to bring Amelia down, as she was certain she'd let the cat out of the bag.'

'Amelia knew too?' Daisy said, shaking her head in disbelief, though it was good natured. She loved knowing she had friends Theo trusted enough to share his secret with.

'So, here is the couple of the hour.' Daisy's mum came and slipped her arm straight between Daisy and Theo, shifting them apart so she could slide into the gap. 'You know, I didn't know if I was going to get to speak to you. I didn't realise you had so many friends down here.'

'Yeah, it's certainly a lot more people than have ever been on the *September Rose* before,' Daisy replied, only for her mother to scoff.

'Oh, well, that's not true. You should have seen some of the parties your father and I had back when I first moved into this place. When I had all my old school buddies show up. And people who weren't my buddies too. Those evenings were legendary. Back before the days of noise complaints and that type of thing. Though it didn't make us particularly popular with the old fuddy-duddies.'

Daisy looked past her mother to catch Theo's eye. His look said it all. Pippa never spoke about her time on Wildflower Lock. Even now, when she spent more time there than in her own home, she would clam up whenever Daisy mentioned the time spent in her early years with Daisy's father on the *September Rose*. At any other time, Daisy would have loved to have learned more about this side of her parents, but bringing up her estranged and deceased father at her engagement party to her mother who had probably had too much to drink didn't feel like a good idea.

'Where's Nicholas?' Theo said, redirecting the conversation. 'Is he having fun? I'm looking forward to testing his sloe gin again this year.'

While Theo had asked her mother two direct questions, she didn't answer either of them. Instead, she posed her own.

'That's not what I'm here to talk about. I've got some questions about you and my daughter. Are you ready to hear them?'

Daisy's stomach twisted. Any doubt she'd had that her mother was drunk evaporated. And while she was sure everything she was going to say to Theo would be kind and polite, it wasn't what Daisy wanted to deal with. She herself had barely drunk two glasses of Champagne, given that every time she went to take a sip, someone else came up to talk to them.

'I'm sure you will have plenty of time to ask Theo your questions,' Daisy replied for him. 'Why don't you grab something to eat? You know Kate and Nick have brought over loads of food. Homemade chutneys. Incredible quiches.'

'Incredible?' Pippa said with a sniff. When it came to food, Daisy's mother cooked professionally and therefore had a higher standard than most. Given her current alcohol consumption, Daisy was momentarily worried that she was going to let the neighbours know if she didn't think it was up to standard. But getting her something to eat was still a wise idea and thankfully, the idea of judging someone else's cooking distracted Pippa from interrogating Theo and she slipped out between the pair, leaving Daisy to move into her previous spot. Although, rather than heading immediately for the food, Pippa turned around and pointed a finger at Theo.

'Don't think I've forgotten you,' she said. 'Trust me, we are going to have words.' A moment later, she was walking away and swaying with a motion that had nothing to do with the slight rocking of the boat.

'Sorry about that,' Daisy said with the slightest of sighs. 'Mum's never great when she's had a couple of drinks. I think she's getting worse as she gets older.'

'You know what they say – you can choose your friends, not your family,' Theo replied, kissing Daisy lightly on the head.

'I thought that's what marriage was? Choosing your family?'

Theo tipped his head to the side slightly, and a tight smile twisted up at the corner of his lips.

'Well, I chose right with you,' he said, then kissed her again.

9

The evening wound down a little before midnight. The children that had come with their parents were all asleep, either on the sofa or on one of the beds, and Claire and Bex began washing up as a way to make it clear that it was time for people to get moving. By quarter past twelve, it was just the four of them that remained.

'So, what about tomorrow?' Daisy said to the girls, as she thought through what her plans for the weekend were going to be. Another early morning was the last thing on her mind as she sat on her sofa with a cup of chamomile tea. She was exhausted, what with the walk and the exceptionally late night, but every time she glanced down at her finger and saw the engagement ring sparkling away, she felt a burst of adrenaline that caused her pulse to race and suddenly she felt wide awake again. Somehow, Daisy didn't think the drink was going to be enough to send her to sleep, but she would use whatever help she could get. 'I take it you're not coming up tomorrow evening too?' Daisy said.

Claire and Bex exchanged a look before glancing at Theo and smiling.

'Well, actually, we thought we might stay the full weekend, if that's okay?' Bex said.

'The entire weekend?' Daisy said. 'Then what are we going to do?'

'Well, I think you should probably tell her this part, don't you, Theo?'

Daisy really didn't know what was going on, but she was sure it wasn't just because she was tired. When she looked at Theo, she noticed a peculiar nervousness twinkling in his eye. Much the same as the one she had seen before he had sent her off on her walk. But he couldn't be proposing again. He had already done that. Which meant she had no idea what was making him act that way. Unless she was just imagining it.

'Theo?' Daisy pressed. 'What's going on?'

'Bex and Claire have offered to run the coffee shop for the weekend. I knew you wouldn't want to miss out on any business. Not while the weather's this good.'

'And Johnny,' Claire interrupted. 'We're looking after Johnny while you're away too.'

'So, where are we going?' Daisy asked, wishing they would just give her a straight answer to what seemed to her a very straightforward question. And yet, Theo's nervousness kicked up by yet another notch. She could see it in the way his hands fidgeted on his lap and the way he repeatedly bit down on his bottom lip. It hadn't been her imagination. Theo opened his mouth to speak, but all of a sudden, Daisy didn't need him to. She knew exactly where they were going. The one place that would make him act like this.

'Well, I thought we could go up to Yorkshire,' he said, confirming she was right. They were going to Yorkshire.

Daisy's heart did a double somersault and landed substantially lower than where it had started.

'Yorkshire,' she repeated, still not sure she believed it was true. 'You mean I'm going to meet your mum and dad?'

10

While Bex and Claire stayed on the *September Rose* together so that they could open up the coffee shop early, Daisy and Theo headed back to the *Narrow Escape* with Johnny, although just as Daisy had expected, falling asleep was the last thing on her mind. It was well past 1 a.m. and they were still wide awake, talking about the night and the neighbours and how lovely it had all been. And as she rested her head on Theo's chest, listening to him talk, Daisy couldn't help but keep glancing at the ring that sparkled on her hand.

'Are you sure you like it? If not, I'm happy for us to choose something together, if that's what you'd rather,' Theo said.

Daisy sprang upwards. 'No, I love it. It's perfect. Is it antique?'

'It was my grandmother's,' he said.

A new sense of emotion tightened in Daisy.

'Your grandmother's? Does that mean you've already told your mum and dad?'

'Not yet. I thought we could do it together.'

Since announcing the trip to Yorkshire, where Daisy would finally meet Theo's parents, Theo hadn't brought up his mum and dad again, and neither had Daisy. It didn't feel like the type of conversation they should have in front of the girls, but they had been alone for quite some time and still neither of them had mentioned the impending introductions.

Despite all the time they had been together, Daisy hadn't so much as spoken to Theo's mum or dad on a video call. It was strange, given how well Theo knew Pippa, but they were a different type of family, he had assured her.

'It's not a big deal. We're just not that close,' Theo had told her before. 'Three visits a year is the most I can handle and even then, we only ever do a couple of days. Any more than that and we end up wanting to tear each other apart.'

'Was it always that way?' Daisy had asked. It was a relief to know she wasn't the only one going into the relationship with a slightly dysfunctional family.

'No, we were pretty close growing up, I suppose. Did lots of family trips and that type of thing. I think moving away just made me see things differently. You know, I realised our values weren't aligned any more. It's not a problem. It's just there a people I'd rather spend my time with. Like you.' After that, they had kissed, and Daisy had felt secure that Theo was telling her the truth. After all, it wasn't as if he hadn't tried to introduce them.

They were meant to come down the previous Christmas, and Daisy and Theo had got everything ready, but then three days before they were due to arrive, his parents decided they weren't sure how they would cope on the water, and so hadn't come. Understandably, Theo had been hugely disappointed. That wasn't the only time they were meant to have met, either. Theo had invited Daisy up to Yorkshire for his mum's sixtieth birthday, but it had coincided with Johnny ingesting an entire tub of hot-chocolate mix and needing an emergency trip to the vets. Thankfully, hot chocolate powder isn't poisonous for dogs like dark chocolate and Johnny was fine, but given the hefty bill, there was no way Daisy could justify closing up the shop just to meet her boyfriend's parents. Besides, there was no way Johnny would have been able to make the journey up, the way his stomach responded to all that powder.

But those events were in the past. Johnny was staying with the girls, and she and Theo were definitely heading up the very next day. Nerves fluttered in Daisy as the importance of the event sank in.

'God, I hope they like me.'

'What a ridiculous thing to say,' Theo said, leaning over and kissing her on the lips. 'Anyone who doesn't like you is insane. Besides, it doesn't matter what they think, does it? It matters what I think. And I, Daisy May, am completely and utterly smitten with you.'

11

Theo said he wanted to leave as early as possible to avoid the traffic, but deep down, Daisy suspected it was to stop her fussing about the coffee shop. The girls had run things now and then – on mornings or afternoons when Daisy had had appointments she couldn't get out of. They had even held down the fort for a full day when Daisy had gone with her mother to a doctor's appointment she was worried about, but they'd never opened up on their own before.

Not that there was much that could go wrong. She'd already baked enough cakes to get through the first day, and her mum had said she would bake anything else that was needed and make sure they were well-stocked throughout the entire weekend. It had been a long time since Daisy's mum had cooked for the coffee shop and Claire had said she was perfectly willing to ship up a couple of batches of millionaire's shortbread or carrot cake, but Pippa had insisted.

'And sorry if I said anything inappropriate last night, dear,' her mother said as she hugged Daisy goodbye. 'Nicholas seems to

think I had one too many. Although I didn't think I was too bad,
was I?'

Daisy recalled the way her mother had swayed back and forth
and proclaimed loudly that she thought the quiches were under-
seasoned, but it didn't seem like the right time to bring it up.

'You were fine, Mum,' she said.

At which point, Pippa smiled broadly.

'You need to get going,' Bex said as Daisy broke away from her
mother. 'We're fine here. You have nothing to be nervous about.'

Bex was wearing the striped apron with the embroidered
narrowboat on that Daisy wore as her uniform and the hatch was
already open, with the price board on display for all passers-by to
see, although no one had yet purchased any drinks.

'She's right. Can we please get going?' Theo said. 'We've got a
long drive ahead of us.'

Daisy looked at her friends, her mother, and then finally to
Johnny, who was sitting on the ground by Claire's feet.

'Just be a good boy, okay? No trouble?'

The dog wagged his tail hard against the ground as Daisy
offered him a tight squeeze, before standing up and turning to
face Theo.

'Okay, then. I guess it's time we got going.'

12

Bex was right. There was no reason for Daisy to be nervous. Not about the coffee shop, at least. Meeting Theo's family, though, that was a whole different matter.

'Okay, what do I need to know?' Daisy said as they hit the motorway. They still had a solid four-hour drive ahead of them until they arrived in Yorkshire, and Daisy wanted to put it to good use, making sure she made the best impression on Theo's family as possible.

With his eyes on the road, Theo let out a slight hum before he spoke.

'Okay, well, don't get into politics with my dad. That's the first thing.'

'He's into politics?'

'He is, and he thinks that it should be the number-one priority in everyone's life.'

Daisy thought about the comment for a moment. 'I guess it is kind of important. We do need to know what's going on in the country we live in. And it's obviously useful to know what's going on in the rest of the world too.'

'Oh, yes, I'm not disagreeing with that,' Theo said. 'But Dad's passion goes way beyond there. You bring up the slightest thing and he'll start telling you when these laws were first put in place and what regulations other countries follow instead. Trust me, politics is not something you want to get into with him. Plus, if he disagrees with your viewpoint in the slightest, he'll spend the rest of our visit trying to convince you you're wrong.'

'Okay...' Daisy said, now understanding why Theo had said it was a subject she needed to steer clear of. 'What should I talk to him about instead?'

Theo pondered the question. 'Birds,' he said finally.

'Birds?'

'Yup. Dad loves birds. I got him one of those camera boxes last Christmas. You know, where you can watch while a bird builds their nest. Something laid eggs in it. A blue tit, I think it was. Anyway, he can talk for hours about that. Not that you need to worry; you just have to be yourself. They'll love you just as you are.'

Daisy smiled at the comment as she considered the topic of birds a little longer. A few years ago, she wouldn't have known where to start. Even when she had moved to Wildflower Lock, she had struggled to tell the difference between an egret and a cormorant. But now, she could talk at length about the various birds of prey and waterfowl that lived on the canal. Yes, she would do well talking to Theo's dad about birds.

'Okay, so what about your mum? What do I need to know there? Is she into birds too?'

'My mum? God, no. That'd hardly be her number-one topic of conversation.'

'So what would be?'

Daisy glanced at Theo and noted the way he was staring at the road ahead of him. His hands were gripping the steering wheel unusually tightly. Of course, it was probably about the traffic and driving on the motorway. It wasn't something they did very often now that he was back living in Wildflower Lock.

'To be honest, I don't know. You're just going to have to judge the conversation when you get there, I'm afraid. Mum's one of those women with a hundred different hobbies. One minute she's into quilting, the next she's taken a lead role in the village amateur dramatics performance, and then two weeks later she'll be helping with the WI, making jams and chutneys for their latest shows.'

'So she likes cooking, then?' Daisy said, grateful to have found a commonality she could use, although surprisingly, Theo shook his head.

'No, she hates cooking.'

'But you said she makes chutney?'

'If the WI wants chutney. Mum's one of those people who can't be left out of any situation. That's why she does all these different hobbies: to make sure she's always included.'

'Oh,' Daisy said, not sure how else she was supposed to reply to such a comment. It didn't sound exactly complimentary.

'I think it's a retirement thing,' Theo replied. 'She wasn't like it when we were growing up. Or at least I don't remember her being like it. But when retirement hit, she suddenly found herself without a way to spend her time and started taking up all these hobbies, and she hasn't stopped.'

'She was a teacher, right?' Daisy said, trying to recall what Theo had previously told her about his family. 'Or was that your dad?'

'Sort of. They were lecturers,' Theo explained. 'Dad lectured in politics. No surprise there. Mum in history. Though she took early retirement years ago.'

'History?' Daisy tried to recall what she could from her school years, sitting at the graffiti-covered tables in her history class. Her teacher had been addicted to dictation, she remembered that much. Lessons were all spent sitting in silence, with the students scribbling away as fast as their wrists could manage, trying to make sure they didn't miss a single date or name. It was fair to say Daisy didn't have the fondest memories of history, and she had dropped it before she even hit GCSE level. She would probably have to find other conversations to have with Theo's mother, and given all the various artistic hobbies she enjoyed, they were bound to have some similar interests. Weren't they?

It didn't take long before the effect of the late night was taking a toll and Daisy found herself struggling to keep her eyes open, but the last thing she wanted to do was fall asleep and leave Theo driving all that way with no one to talk to and so she struggled on, chatting away, turning the volume on the radio up extra loud so that she didn't drift off. And for a while, it worked, until a couple of hours into the trip, when they stopped off at a cute farm shop for something to eat. Afterwards, with the weight of the food sitting in her stomach, and the warmth of the sun beating through the windows and heating the car, Daisy found her eyes feeling heavy. It was too much. She just needed a quick twenty-minute nap. That was what she told Theo. A quick nap and she would be fine. And so she let her eyes close.

'Hey you.' Theo's hand rocked her gently on the shoulder.

A sound that was something between a yawn and a groan escaped Daisy's mouth as she finally pushed herself up straight.

'Wow, I needed that.'

'I figured as much,' Theo replied.

Still yawning, Daisy blinked a couple of times until her vision finally focused, and she was surprised to find they were no longer on the motorway. In fact, they were no longer on a road of any sort. Instead, they were parked up outside a large gate, which lead to a private road.

'I hope you're feeling well-rested,' Theo said as he leaned across and kissed her lips. 'Because it's time for you to meet my parents.'

13

Daisy wasn't cross with Theo; she couldn't be. Only the night before, he had proposed to her in a more romantic manner than she could have ever dreamt of, but she wished she had had just a little more preparation for meeting his parents. She should have brought something with her – a cake, perhaps, or one of the pecan tarts she had been making recently for the café. They had been flying off the shelf and would have been a perfect gift. Instead, she was turning up with a bottle of wine that someone had left on the boat the night before. Fingers crossed it was a good one.

'I just wish I could get changed first,' Daisy said, wishing she hadn't worn a material that crumpled so much for such a long journey. 'And are you sure they don't mind us staying at theirs? We could get a hotel.'

'Really, you are fussing about nothing. Look, they might take a bit of time to warm up to you, but once they see how much I love you, they're going to be just as smitten with you as I am,' Theo said.

Daisy knew the words were meant to comfort her. They didn't.

'What do you mean, "take a bit of time to warm up"? Why will they need to warm up to me? Do they know things about me already? Is it because I didn't go to university? Are they the type of people who only like you if you've got a proper education? What am I saying? Of course they are. They're bloody lecturers.'

'Will you stop?' Theo said, reaching across and placing his hand on her knee. 'There is nothing about you that my parents shouldn't love. I'm just warning you that they can be a bit peculiar. A bit standoffish sometimes.'

Daisy was feeling worse and worse.

'What do you mean, peculiar? Standoffish? I need examples. Do they know things about me? Like about Christian? Is that why they don't like me? Because I didn't know what I was thinking before we first got together? Or was it the trip around London? They think I'm irresponsible, don't they? That I'm a bad influence on you? Oh God. This is going to be terrible. It is, I can feel it.'

'For goodness' sake.' Theo snatched his hand off Daisy's knee and took her firmly by the shoulders, and swivelled her around in her seat so that she was looking directly at him. 'Daisy, I want you to remember one thing and one thing only: I love you. I love you so much that I want to spend the rest of my life with you and no one else, and I'm hoping that you feel the same way.'

'I do,' Daisy said, though her heart was beating so fast at the impending disaster of meeting his parents, she was almost breathless.

'Then that is all that matters. Nothing else matters. I said my parents can be a bit peculiar because they can. They're the type of people who still think everyone else should know the difference between a smoking jacket and a dinner jacket.'

'What the hell is a smoking jacket? Is that even a thing?' Daisy said, the panic surging once again. 'Should I have one? Are they something women wear too?'

'Daisy, listen!' Theo's sharp voice brought her back to the moment. 'I moved hundreds of miles to be away from my family and I moved hundreds of miles to be back close to you. Do you understand what I'm trying to say?'

'You've moved a lot around the country?' Daisy said, almost sure that wasn't the right answer.

'No,' Theo replied. 'It means that their lifestyle, and the way they sometimes act, isn't what I want to be around. You are. You are it for me, Daisy. I want you to meet them because they are my family, the people who raised me. They are the ones who shaped so much of who I am. And you? You are going to be the person I spend the rest of my life with. Who will shape my future and the person I will become. It makes sense that you should meet. But at the end of the day, this weekend could go perfectly or be a complete and utter disaster, and it wouldn't change how I feel about you, okay? You are the one I love. The one I intend to live with until I'm old and grey. Got it?'

The loud sigh which followed indicted that Theo had come to the end of his speech, though he looked at her as if he were expecting an answer, but Daisy still wasn't sure what she was meant to reply. All she had really got from the conversation was that there was a very good chance Theo's parents weren't going to like her, and she just had to suck it up until they could get back to Wildflower Lock, and it would just be the two of them again.

'I guess so?' she said, not sure what else to say.

With a smile and a look of relief on his face, Theo kissed her lightly on the cheek before turning his attention back to the car.

'Great. Then it's time we got this show on the road.'

14

Daisy wasn't sure where she had expected Theo's parents to live, other than the Lake District. In her imagination, everyone who resided in the Lake District lived in an idyllic cottage, on the top of a rolling hill, with a view out over acres and acres of lush green fields that stretched into vibrant blue lakes. And she had got some parts correct. The house *was* on top of a hill, and it was probably idyllic, although it was currently difficult to tell. Despite having driven in through the large gate over a minute before-hand, they were still trundling down a tree-lined driveway with no hint of a house in sight.

'Are they the only people who live down here?' Daisy asked, looking around for any sign of life. 'Or are there lots of houses down here?'

'It's just their place,' Theo said. 'Although they might have a lodger. They sometimes do that when they get fed up with each other's company. Or when one of Mum's friends decides she's leaving her husband again. She's had a few of those camp out for a month or so before. Actually, I think Dad has too. But I don't think there's anyone staying with them at the moment.'

Lodgers and people staying with them for over a month? Daisy loved having Bex and Claire stay. She'd had Amelia over at times too, but even though the *September Rose* was a spacious, wide beam canal boat, squeezing them all in for two nights was as much as Daisy could cope with. It was the same when she'd had the flat. Bex would often stay on her sofa, but after two nights, they would feel on top of one another. She struggled to imagine how big Theo's parents' place would have to be for that not to be an issue, though it didn't take her long to find out.

'This can't be where you grew up,' Daisy said breathlessly as the house finally came into view.

The long driveway opened up into a large gravel space, upon which stood a single white house. Well, Daisy assumed it was a single house, given the conversation they had just had, but it was easily four times the size of the one Daisy grew up in. The roof was covered in dark slate tiles, and with just a quick glance, she counted five chimneys. How was it possible, she thought, that a house needed so many chimneys? With the air in her lungs feeling decidedly thin, she continued to take in the building. A series of steps led up to the front door, around which the spindly branches of a wisteria draped, the last of its purple blooms fading. Two of the windows were made of stained glass and depicted hills and lakes. There was something about the composition and colour that led Daisy to believe they were real places.

'You grew up here?' Daisy said, transfixed not only by the house but by the land that stretched around it. Manicured lawns with perfectly pruned rose hedges and bushes, interspersed with ornate flower beds. Three cars were parked out front, one of which was a sports car and another a 4x4.

'I did,' Theo said. 'And believe me, no matter how big it looks, it can get pretty claustrophobic inside.'

Daisy considered the remark slightly odd but paid it little

mind as she stepped out of the car and onto the driveway. Despite it being later in the day, it was far chillier up here than it had been when they left Wildflower Lock.

'I should grab my cardigan from the back,' she said, moving towards the boot of the car, but Theo caught her.

'Don't worry, we can get everything in afterwards in a moment. It's probably better if we get straight into the house. Dad has a thing about people standing outside and dawdling.'

Daisy didn't think that getting a cardigan to ensure she wasn't freezing counted as dawdling, but she was already worried about making a less-than-ideal impression, and so she took Theo's advice and walked towards the door.

'Are you shaking because you're cold or because you're nervous?' he said as he took her hand, then wrapped an arm around her to rub her shoulder.

'A bit of both,' Daisy replied truthfully.

'Well, don't be nervous, honestly. We're just here for one night. I've got an exciting night planned for us tomorrow elsewhere.'

Daisy looked at Theo in surprise, the current situation momentarily forgotten.

'We're not staying here tomorrow?'

'I thought perhaps we deserved something a bit romantic for the weekend after our engagement, don't you? Unless, of course, you want to stay here?'

Daisy looked back at the house. It was hard to imagine a more romantic destination, but given all the effort Theo had gone to, there was no way she was going to say that.

'A romantic night away anywhere with you sounds absolutely perfect,' Daisy said as she pushed herself up onto her tiptoes and planted a kiss firmly on Theo's lips. She had intended it to be nothing more than a peck, but as his hand slipped around her waist, she found herself leaning more into him. Given how he had been driving all day, she barely had time to stop and kiss him or revel in the fact that he was indeed her fiancé. As such, the kiss was one she could have lost herself in for several more minutes, had the front door to the house not swung open.

'At last, Theodore. We were expecting you hours ago,' a pristinely dressed woman said from the doorway. Every inch of her was exact, from the gentle curls of her hair to the perfect points of her shoes, although it was her expression that held Daisy's attention the most. With a slight pout, she looked Daisy up and down so slowly that it wasn't even subtle, and when she stopped and locked her gaze on Daisy's, her smile tightened ever so slightly.

'So,' she said, with a voice that was both breathy and yet direct. 'You must be the wonderful Maisy I've heard so much about.'

15

Daisy blinked and opened her mouth as if to reply, but she wasn't sure what to say. She had misheard, surely? Theo's mother hadn't just called her the wrong name, had she? Swallowing back the fear that was flooding through her, she was still trying to believe it was her mistake when Theo spoke.

'It's Daisy, as you well know. Daisy with a D.'

'Oh, yes, well, you know what it's like with these modern names. They're all far too easy to confuse, aren't they?'

Her smile widened as she looked at Daisy again, although there was no warmth to it at all. Everything from the bright blue of her eyes to her narrowed lips screamed ice queen. Any hope Daisy had had of a warm welcome was rapidly fading.

'Daisy, this is my mother, Penelope. Or Penny, if it's a good day,' Theo said.

Daisy's immediate thought was that Penny didn't sound any less modern a name than Daisy, but she kept that to herself as she smiled.

'Penny, so pleased to meet you.' She stretched out her right hand.

'Really, Penelope is fine. Why Theodore insists on only using half the name we gave him is beyond me.'

'Right, sorry, Penelope,' Daisy said. Her hand was still outstretched, but after a moment longer, she realised it wasn't going to be met and lowered it to her side.

A bit of time to warm up? Wasn't that what Theo had said about his parents? Judging by their encounter so far, Daisy doubted that even several hours on defrost in a high-powered microwave would be enough to thaw Penelope out.

'Is that Theo? Tell him to come inside and stop dawdling.'

The booming voice came from deep inside the house and was shortly followed by the appearance of a large man wearing a checked shirt, green trousers and a strained waistcoat struggling to remain buttoned up.

'Come on, lad, let's get those bags of yours inside. Don't want you letting all the warm air out, do we?'

Daisy couldn't imagine how hot it would have to be inside the house for it to be warmer than outside, but this felt like something to keep to herself, so instead she turned to Theo.

'I'll go get the bags,' she said. 'You stay here with your mum and dad. You've got lots to catch up on.'

She could see from Theo's face that he was about to refuse, but the look she gave was all it took for him to nod quickly in agreement. Still, when she turned to walk to the car, she quickly heard him speak again.

'Actually, I think some of those bags are quite heavy. It's probably best if I give her a hand too,' he said. 'We'll just be one second. We'll take our bags up to the guest room and then come down to the kitchen. I think we'd both love a cup of tea.'

When Daisy turned back towards the house, her eyes fell on Theo's mother, who was pouting with such force, her entire cheeks were drawn inwards.

'Fine,' Penelope said with a huffiness that made it sound like Theo helping Daisy was the worst thing he could possibly offer to do. 'But try not to trample mud through the house. You know how your father abhors having to vacuum more than three times a week.'

16

It was only when Theo's parents disappeared into the house that Daisy let out a long sigh of relief that sounded more like a gasp. A moment later, Theo was standing by her side, taking her hands.

'Well, I guess I know what you mean about standoffish,' Daisy said. Now that she was away from the situation, the conversation they'd just had was starting to sink in. 'She did that on purpose, didn't she? Calling me the wrong name?'

Theo paused. A slight cough caught in his throat before he released it as a groan.

'I'm sorry. I'd love to give her the benefit of the doubt, but I did say there was a reason I lived so far away.' He shook his head and let out a groan even longer than the first one. 'I honestly thought introducing you was the right thing to do, so we could tell her about the engagement together, but she's much better when there are more people. I should have thought about that. I mean, I'm sure she'll get better. It's a defence mechanism, you know? Mum always has to feel like she's got one over on you. I have no idea why, but after that, she tends to mellow out a bit. But if it's going to be too difficult, we don't have to stay.' As he looked down at Daisy, a sense of sadness and disappointment filled his eyes. 'I can ring the hotel. See if they can squeeze us in for an extra night.'

Daisy was torn. In her opinion, Penelope needed to do a lot more than mellow to become anywhere near palatable. After all, who aimed to get things over on people they didn't even know? Certainly not the type of person she would choose to spend any time with. But however strong a dislike she had taken to the woman, she was still Theo's mother, and he wouldn't have brought her there to meet his family unless it was important to him.

'No, it's fine,' Daisy said, trying to project an inner strength and positivity she didn't feel. 'I'm sure she was just nervous about meeting me, too. I mean, she's bound to be a bit wary of this girl her son moved back around the country for. Especially when they've never even met me.'

'Exactly,' Theo said, relief washing over his face. 'I'm sure when we tell them about the engagement, they'll be over the moon, just you wait and see.'

Excitement returned to Theo's face and with it, a sense of optimism in Daisy. It had been a rough introduction, that was all. And it wasn't like she and Theo had had the best first meeting. Yes, the more she thought about it, the more she decided that the old line about first impressions wasn't really true at all. Theo's parents would love her and she would love them, too. She was sure of it.

As she slung her bag over her shoulder and slipped her hand into Theo's, she looked up at him and frowned.

'Did they say we are sleeping in the guest bedroom? Is that what they did to your room after you moved out?' she said. 'Made it for guests?'

Rather than replying normally, as Daisy had expected Theo to do, he let out a loud scoff.

'Oh no, the guest wing has always been there. They turned my room into storage for Mum's dress-making and Dad's golf clubs.'

17

The inside of the house was every bit the country chic that Daisy had imagined from the outside.

Dark oak flooring in the hallway gave way to a tiled-floor kitchen, where duck-egg blue counter tops were fashioned in a traditional style, with an Aga nestled at one end and a large dining table in the centre. The windows were deep-set and white-washed, accented with small roller blinds, whilst large troughs filled with herbs sat on the windowsill. It was the type of house Daisy had dreamed of, when she first thought of growing up, getting married and having children. The type of house where you could hear the thunder of feet on the floorboards above you and rattles of laughter as siblings chased one another up and down the staircase and around the copious garden. It was the type of kitchen where she could have imagined propping a little one up on a stool and teaching her to make scones and cakes, the way her mother had done for her. A house filled with laughter and love. That was what it felt like this house should have been, yet at that moment, it felt as if both those aspects were thoroughly missing.

'I take it the drive was all right?' Theo's father asked. Daisy was well aware that they hadn't yet been introduced, but given that he had made no attempt to speak to her, she wasn't sure whether she wanted to extend any form of greeting. Instead, she lingered behind Theo, like she was some terrified schoolgirl, not a grown businesswoman who was meeting her fiancé's family.

'Traffic was good, actually. We left early. Thankfully, Daisy's used to the early mornings, what with the coffee shop and everything.'

Daisy smiled gratefully at Theo for trying to include her in the conversation, but before she could comment, Penelope was speaking again.

'Ahh, yes. You're a waitress, isn't that right?'

'No, I'm not,' Daisy replied tersely, only to see the flicker of satisfaction on Penelope's lips. Of course she knew Daisy wasn't a waitress. She was goading her and Daisy had stupidly bitten, but she wasn't going to let Penelope get the last laugh and so she continued, 'I have to say, I have great admiration for wait staff, though. I know how difficult some of the people I have to deal with as the owner of the coffee shop can be. And that's only take-away. I can't imagine how tough it must be when you're stuck serving rude, entitled customers on a table you can't get away from.' She locked her eyes on Penelope as she said this last line, making it entirely clear who she was talking about. As Theo's mother pouted, Daisy smiled as broadly and warmly as she could. 'But I happen to love my job, running my own business, which is doing incredibly well, actually. I'm very lucky.'

If it was possible to hear someone's teeth grinding together, Daisy was certain she would have done, as Penelope's lips twitched and pursed as if she was having to stop herself from snarling. A paused elongated between them, and Daisy was sure she was about to bite back, but instead, Penelope offered her only a beaming smile.

'Well, then, I'm sure this weekend will be quite the relaxation you need. Now, I'll put the kettle on. Was it tea or coffee you wanted?'

'I'll have—'

'Actually, Mum,' Theo said, cutting across Daisy before she could speak, 'the drive over was really hot and sweaty. Daisy and I were just saying how we'd like to grab a shower before we have a drink. You don't mind, do you?'

Penelope's smile twisted, tightening and contorting as she peered down her nose.

'Of course not, darling. This is your home. You may do as you wish.'

'Thank you.'

'There are spare towels on your bed. Try not to get them too dirty.'

18

Daisy had to bite her tongue. Who made a comment about making towels dirty? And what did Penelope think she and Theo had been doing on the drive over? Stopping to have a mudbath? Still, Daisy had already been far less polite than she would ever normally dreamed possible. What she needed to do was try to make amends.

'I'm sorry,' Daisy said the moment they were out of earshot. 'I know I was rude to her, only she was so condescending. The way she said the word *waitress*. Like waitresses don't work damn hard.'

Theo nodded as he looked down at Daisy and placed a hand on her cheek.

'I know. I get it. I understand how difficult she can be, but the thing with my mum is—'

'She's your mum, I get it,' Daisy said, anticipating what Theo was going to say next. 'She's your mum and you love her and I'll learn to love her too if I just give her a chance. I get it. I do. And I'll try. I promise.'

Theo paused and pressed his lips together.

'Actually, that wasn't what I was going to say at all.'

'It wasn't?' Daisy frowned.

'No, I was going to say that she just has to feel like she's winning. That's it. She has to have the last word with everything. And as much as I love to see you standing up to her – and believe me, I do love to see you standing up to her – the last thing I want is for her to decide she's going to use that against you. You know, start being unpleasant.'

'*Start* being unpleasant?' Daisy said. 'Did you listen to anything she said?'

'I know, I get it.' Theo took her hands and squeezed them tightly. 'It's probably not going to make you feel any better, but she's exactly the same with my sister. Always trying to get under her skin. You have every right to answer back and give her everything she deserves, but it's just you I'm worried about. I'm worried about how difficult she can make things for us.'

'We're only staying here for one night,' Daisy said, although she knew deep down that wasn't what Theo was on about. They were getting married. That meant that whether she liked it or not, Penelope was in her life for good now.

'Please, just this once, can you try to take the higher ground with her?' As he spoke, Theo pushed out his bottom lip and offered Daisy his best puppy-dog eyes that were so good, even Johnny would have a hard time topping them. 'I'll promise I'll make it up to you when we go to the hotel,' he added.

'Really? And how do you plan on doing that?'

Leaning forward, Theo whispered into Daisy's ear, causing her to let out an uncontrollable burst of laughter.

'Fine then, you're on. But I'm holding you to that.'

'Good,' Theo said with a grin that was wide enough to make Daisy's heart flutter. 'I want you to.'

19

Unlike her personality, everything about Penelope's guest room was fluffy. The throw cushions were fluffy, the towels were fluffy and there was even a fluffy teddy bear sat in the middle of the cushions, while the carpet was the densest Daisy had ever stood on. It was undeniably sumptuous and the opulence didn't stop in the bedroom. The en suite shower was filled with the most luxurious brands of soap, shower gel and bodywash, and Penelope had even gone as far as to lay out little guest toothbrushes, like the types given out at hotels. It was hard to believe that someone who had gone to all that effort would be so vile to her guests, but then, Daisy considered, maybe she had read her wrong. Maybe Penelope had really thought her name was Maisy, and that she was a waitress. If Theo didn't speak to her that often, then it stood to reason that she would make a couple of mistakes.

'Was your mum like this to Heather?' Daisy asked as she took a clean dress out of her luggage and hung it on a coat hanger. 'Did she act strangely to her?'

Theo barely pondered the question. Instead, he simply scrunched up his nose before he spoke.

'It was different with Heather. You know, with us growing up together and everything,' he said.

'What do you mean?' Daisy asked. 'I didn't realise you two grew up together. Did you go to the same school? Is that what you mean?'

'Well, we did, but it was more than that. Heather's mum has been best friends with my parents for years. They've known each other their entire lives. I think Heather and I even went to the same baby groups together.'

Daisy dropped down onto the bed, feeling a sudden weight flooding through her.

'How did I not know that?' she said. 'I knew you'd been together for a long time, but surely that's something I should have known?'

A deep furrow formed between Theo's brows. 'I don't know. I guess I didn't think it was much of a big deal. We didn't get together until after we'd both left home. We were only ever friends until then. But I suppose that's why I had such a hard time finishing things. We both did, because we knew how difficult it was going to be on our families as well.'

Daisy stared off into the distance as she tried to make sense of what she'd just heard. Did it really matter that Theo and Heather had known each other that long? Or that his parents probably thought about her as a daughter? It shouldn't, and on one hand it didn't. Heather was Theo's past and she was his future, but it was the fact she hadn't known any of this that left her feeling uneasy. To start with, she'd have been far more understanding of Penelope's reaction. Part of her wanted to be cross with Theo for not filling her in on the full picture, but then again, did Theo know everything about her and Paul? Probably not.

'So, I guess if your parents are still friends, then she's always going to be in your life, in a way,' Daisy said, imagining a wedding with Penelope sat on one side of the top table, and Heather on the other, speaking across Daisy as if she were invisible. Panic tightened her chest.

As if sensing the feeling, Theo reached around and took her arm.

'It's nothing to worry about, honestly. You don't need to worry about Heather, and you don't need to worry about my mum. It's you and me, always, Daisy May, okay?'

She nodded, although the knot in her stomach remained.

'Come on,' Theo said. 'Let's go down and get a cup of tea. I'm parched.'

20

Downstairs, a pot of tea was waiting on the kitchen island, along with a tin of flapjacks and a packet of shortbread rounds.

'Not homemade,' Penelope said with that same tight-lipped smile. 'But they are from the farmers' market and they do make everything fresh, with organic ingredients. I can't remember... is your little café organic, Daisy?'

Daisy drew in a long breath as she forced her lips into a smile.

'Of course,' she said, knowing it probably wasn't true. It wasn't like Penelope was ever going to come down and see for herself.

'Well, shall we take the tea into the drawing room?' Penelope continued, as if she hadn't even asked Daisy a question, let alone heard Daisy's reply. 'We don't want to sit out here in the kitchen, do we? Theo, can you take the tray, please? Daisy can help me with the plates.'

There was no question in her sentence, and so Daisy instinctively moved to pick up the large set of plates set on the counter, but no sooner had she moved than Penelope barked at her.

'No, not those, Daisy. Not for biscuits. Archibald, get Daisy the proper plates.'

Daisy pressed her lips together, trying to suppress a smirk. Being named Archibald was one thing; having your wife use it was another. Penelope sounded like she was ordering around a child.

The drawing room was, like the rest of the house, exactly as Daisy had expected: an outdated cliché of how the wealthy would dress their rooms, with a miniature grand piano in one corner, and velvet curtains with large drapes folding down. A large pink rug sat on the faded carpet and none of the furniture matched, with a floral sofa, two large leather armchairs and several small tub chairs.

After Theo had placed the tea tray on the coffee table, Daisy put the plates down next to it before taking a seat and allowing Penelope the room to pour the drinks.

'I didn't bring sugar, but I assume no one will need it,' she said. 'I do not understand people who suffocate the taste of tea with sugar, do you, Daisy?'

'Well, I let my customers choose how they want their drinks,' Daisy replied. 'I'm not sure they'd pay me for them otherwise.'

'Of course, of course you do,' Penelope said, fixing them all identical drinks with milk and no sugar. When everyone had a cup of tea, Theo's mother took a seat in one of the tub chairs, but despite the softness of the fabric, she looked anything but relaxed. The way she placed her hands upon her knees reminded Daisy of a poster she'd seen from the 1940s, demonstrating all the good qualities a wife should have. She didn't know whether she should laugh or cry.

'Well, this trip was a welcome surprise,' Theo's father said, as he helped himself simultaneously to a shortbread and a piece of flapjack, seemingly able to ignore Penelope's glare. 'I have to say, we were talking only the other day about how long it's been since we've seen you. Not that we're not pleased, but is there any particular reason that you've graced us with your presence today?'

Daisy's heart began hammering in her chest. She had assumed telling people about her engagement would be exciting. That it would be the type of moment when people would sweep around you and congratulate you, pat you on the back, and say how excited they were for you. But she had the distinct impression that it wouldn't be that way today. She glanced at Theo, wondering if he was going to say anything, and it was only then she realised she had kept her hands folded the entire time, the antique ring tucked out of view.

As she held Theo's gaze, he offered her a warm smile before reaching out and taking her hand.

'Actually, there is. We have a bit of news to share.'

Daisy didn't want to look at Theo's parents' faces. She wanted to keep her eyes on him only, but she knew that couldn't happen. Steeling her breath, she slipped her hand out of his, displaying the ring in all its beauty.

'Theo asked me to marry him. And I said yes.'

She waited for the snarky comment, the cutting remarks that made Daisy feel less than two inches tall. But instead, Penelope smiled broadly, her face beaming as she reached forward and took Daisy's hand in hers.

'Oh, I'm so pleased,' she said.

'You are?' Daisy and Theo spoke simultaneously.

'Yes, I've been so worried that you lost that ring after you asked for it to give to Heather. Tell me, Theo, you did give that ring to her when you proposed then, didn't you?'

21

Daisy wanted the floor to swallow her up. No, she *needed* the floor to swallow her up, because the only other options were storming out of the room, having some very choice words for her fiancé with his parents there watching, or bursting into tears. And she had a horrible feeling that she was closest to the latter.

She swallowed hard repeatedly, feeling Penelope's eyes boring into her, but what was she supposed to say? That she knew Theo had already used this ring to propose once? And that she didn't mind? She'd have had a hard time sounding truthful, considering she hadn't even known that Theo and Heather had ever been engaged before. Besides, at that moment, Daisy wasn't even sure she could speak. Once again, she attempted to swallow down the lump that had lodged itself up in her throat, but before she managed to clear it, Theo was speaking.

'Heather and I didn't get engaged, Mother, as you know,' Theo said. His voice sounded remarkably calm and at any other time, it might have put Daisy at ease. But Penelope's smile only broadened, and it had the same effect on Daisy as nails on a chalkboard. A cold shudder ran down her spine.

'Yes, darling, of course. I'm sorry. I didn't mean to bring that up.' Penelope looked at Daisy. 'She rejected him, you know, but good thing too, or else you wouldn't have that pretty little ring on your finger, would you?'

That was it. Daisy couldn't take any more. Tears of betrayal were clogging her throat. She needed to get out of the room and fast, but she didn't want it to look like Penelope had won. She hadn't. None of her tears were for Penelope. It was the fact that there was yet another omission by Theo – another part of his life that Theo had kept from her – that hurt so badly.

In as controlled a manner as she could, she stood up and smiled graciously.

'Sorry, if you don't mind, I'm just going to get some water. I think the organic flapjacks needed another ten minutes in the oven. They're somewhat undercooked and a little cloying.'

With that, she walked out of the room.

22

The minute she was out of the drawing room, Daisy picked up the pace, running at a near sprint through the rest of the house as she headed to the front door. She didn't want to be in this house any longer. She didn't want to be surrounded by the antiquated furniture and the fancy side plates. What she needed was air. Lots and lots of it.

With her breath staggered, she pushed open the door and ran out into the driveway.

'Daisy, wait.' Her feet had barely crunched on the gravel when Theo was outside too and a second later, he had his hand on her shoulder. 'Please, Daisy, wait.'

It was more through disbelief than anything else that she stopped in her tracks, with her heart pounding. Even when Theo dropped his hand, she didn't move.

With her hands clenched at her side, Daisy could feel Theo's presence right behind her. It almost felt as if she could see the expression on his face too. The pained concern with which he was viewing her, but Daisy didn't turn and face him. She couldn't. Angry tears were pricking her eyes. Angry tears she wanted to swallow back down. Either that, or spit them back at Theo. A moment later, that was the option she chose.

'Is it true?' she said, swivelling around so she could look him in the eye. 'Is it true, you proposed to Heather with the same ring as you gave me? Crap, I don't even know what I'm more upset about – the fact you gave me the same freaking ring, or the fact that you didn't even tell me you and Heather got engaged.'

'We didn't get engaged,' Theo said, stressing his words, though if they were meant to bring Daisy any relief, they didn't. Instead, they only caused a bitter cough to escape from her throat.

'No, sorry, I forgot that part. She turned you down when you proposed with this ring. I guess that's one way to save money. Just use the hand-me-down on the next fool who's stupid enough to say yes to you.'

As she stopped, she looked up at Theo, although she had barely met his gaze when he lowered it to the ground.

'You don't mean that, do you?' he said. 'You don't think you're a fool for wanting to marry me? Or that I just gave you that ring because I had it hanging around and wasn't sure what else to do with it?'

Daisy didn't know how to reply. Less than twenty-four hours ago, she had thought she was going to marry the man of her dreams. Now she wasn't even sure if that man existed.

'I don't understand, Theo. I don't...' Her words were strained, tight from the tears that clogged her throat.

'I know. I know you don't. Please, can you just let me explain? Just let me tell you what happened?'

Daisy felt a sharp sting inside her mouth and only then did she realise she was chewing on the inside of her cheek, while her hands were still clenched so tightly, her nails dug into her palms.

Still trying to control her shuddering breaths, she lifted her head and looked up towards the house.

'I'm not going back in there,' she said. 'I can't. I don't ever want to look at your mother again. You know she enjoyed that?'

'I get it. I do. But we can talk out here. In the garden. Or in the car? Why don't we sit in the car and talk?'

Daisy wasn't sure if she wanted to talk. She wasn't even sure if she could. But then she wasn't the one who had to. It was Theo who needed to talk. Who needed to explain why he had just caused her more humiliation and hurt than any single person had ever done. She just needed to decide if she wanted to listen.

Daisy glanced down at the ring on her hand that only moments ago had felt like such a symbol of love and loyalty. Now, though, it felt like a symbol of betrayal.

'Fine,' she said, dipping her chin to offer him the tiniest of nods. 'We can talk in the car.'

23

Daisy took the driver's seat. She wasn't sure why it mattered, really. Yes, it was her car, but Theo had driven all the way up here and used it almost as often as she did now. But it was where she needed to sit. Perhaps so that she could switch on the engine and make a run for it if she didn't like what he had to say.

Given how keen Theo had been to speak, silence enveloped them as they sat there. Still Daisy waited, yet every time he opened his mouth as if he were going to speak, he closed it again. Soon, she couldn't take it any longer.

'So, you did propose to Heather with the ring then,' Daisy said, seeing no point in beating around the bush. 'You proposed, she said no, then you moved on to me. That's right, isn't it?'

'No.' Theo shook his head. 'And you know it's not. You know I chose you. Even when Heather came back to me asking for another try, I told her it was you. I told her you were the only person I wanted to be with. Even though you were stringing me along at the time, you might remember?'

Daisy refused to respond. There was no way she was going to be made out as the villain in this. She had owned up to her mistakes at the beginning of the relationship and thought they were past them. And Theo had assured her he was, although now he seemed to be using any reason to detract attention from him.

A pause stretched out between them and Daisy was about to tell him she didn't want to hear any more, when Theo suddenly started speaking.

'We'd been together for about two years. I had taken the job on the lock and she had got this big promotion in London. One that involved loads of travelling, meaning I would go weeks at a time without seeing her. I got paranoid. Worried she was going to discover this whole new life, probably with one of her swanky male colleagues she used to talk about. Men who sounded like they had a lot more to offer to her than some guy working on the canals. So I did what I thought was right – I proposed to her. It felt like a way to keep her close. You have to remember, I was young and paranoid, and she was the only girl I had ever loved.'

'So you gave Heather the ring, and then what?' Daisy had a hard time believing this was where the story ended and she wasn't even going to think about how to respond until she knew everything.

'She just said no and told me I was being ridiculous. That we were far too young to get married and that if a relationship was strong enough, it wouldn't matter. She was right. Everything she said was right.'

'And how did you take that news?' Daisy asked, trying to imagine the situation. She knew how much effort Theo had put into proposing to her and, as much as he was making out that this first proposal wasn't a big deal, she knew him well enough to know he would have still pulled out all the stops.

'How was I?' he said, raising an eyebrow. 'I was pissed off. At first, that is, but not for long. Everything Heather had said was completely true, and I got that. It took maybe a week or so, but honestly, not any longer than that. I don't think she even mentioned the proposal to anyone. I know I didn't. The only reason that Mum and Dad knew about it was because of my grandmother's ring. I'd had to ask them if I could have it, even though my grandmother had always wanted me to use it to propose.'

Daisy glanced down at her hand and the gemstones. Would she ever be able to look at it and not see Theo down on one knee, offering a lifetime's commitment to someone else? She didn't know.

'I don't think Heather even put the ring on her finger,' Theo said, as if he was reading Daisy's mind. 'And I promise you, I truly had forgotten the proposal to Heather. That was how little it meant to me. But the ring... My grandmother and I were close, and I wanted to share that part of my life with you. But I get it, I completely do. If you don't like it, I will get another one, or you can choose another one, or we can go together and get one. I don't care, I just want to put this right somehow. I love you. You do know that I love you, don't you?'

The way his eyes pleaded with Daisy felt like it was tugging directly on every one of her heartstrings.

'Of course I know that,' she said. She knew exactly how much Theo adored her. Just like she knew they would get past this. But that didn't stop how much it hurt. 'I think I'm just going to need a little time to decide, if that's okay?'

Theo's faced turned ashen. 'About the ring or the proposal?' he said.

The moment she heard the question come from her lips, she knew what the answer was.

'Just about the ring,' she said.

For a second, Theo continued to stare at Daisy, his lips slightly parted, as if he didn't quite believe what she was saying.

'So we're good? You still want to marry me? Even after I made the most stupid mistake in the world?'

A slight chuckle left her lips. 'Yes, yes, I do.'

With a loud and nervous laugh that quickly turned into a sigh, Theo dropped his head onto Daisy's shoulder.

'You know I love you more than anything else in the world,' he said as he moved to kiss her, but before he could, Daisy backed away.

'Just one more thing,' she said, placing her hand on his chest.

'Anything, just ask.'

'I really don't want to spend tonight at your parents'. Can you ring that hotel, see if we can check in a night early?'

A look of relief washed over Theo's face.

'God yes. I will do it right now.'

Despite all their pleadings, the hotel didn't have a room for the extra night.

'It's fine. I can just stay in the guest room and out of your parents' way,' Daisy said. 'Or maybe I can just go for a very long walk in the garden and stay outside until they've gone to bed.'

'You'll be hard-pressed to manage that,' Theo replied. 'They're complete night owls. They never go to sleep until they've had several night caps, but...'

He tilted his head to the side, and a slight smile twisted the corner of his lips.

'Theo?' Daisy said, knowing full well that his look meant he had just thought of something.

'I have an idea. Give me a minute, I just need to go into the house and see if I can find something.' He opened the car door and was halfway out when he changed his mind. Climbing back in, he kissed Daisy quickly on the cheek, before leaving for real. 'I won't be long,' he called from the front door.

Ten minutes later, Daisy glanced at her watch. Theo's idea of a minute was obviously substantially longer than hers and yet she wasn't sure what else she could do other than wait. She didn't want to go back into the house and could only imagine how Penelope would react if she stood outside and shouted his name, but she could always phone him. Ringing Theo to see how much longer he was going to be felt like the sensible option. Yet as she looked at the screen and prepared to hit Theo's number, her phone started ringing itself. Only it wasn't Theo calling her. Instead, Bex's name flashed on the screen.

Worried that perhaps something was wrong with the café, Daisy answered.

'Is everything okay?' she asked. 'Has something happened?'

'Wow, now that almost sounds like you don't trust us.' Bex laughed. 'Everything's fine. I just thought I'd give you a quick ring. It has been manic, though. How do you do this five days a week?'

'I don't, I normally do it seven,' Daisy reminded her. 'Well, at least six.'

Bex let out a long blow of air, which buzzed down the phone line.

'You know my respect for you is immense, don't you?'

There was something so factual yet lovely about her friend's remark that it caused a warm feeling to flood through her, but before she could reply, Bex was talking again. 'Now tell me everything. You must be there by now, right? What's his family like? I imagined they'll be the total opposite to Theo, right? Super chill, maybe a bit messy?'

'Oh, they are definitely not chill, or messy,' Daisy said, biting down on her lip as she tried to work out what she should say next. She didn't want to be overly down on Theo, given how they had just smoothed everything over, but she needed some perspective. Bex and Claire both loved Theo. They were hardly likely to take a harsh approach unless he really deserved it.

'So, come—'

'I need to ask you something,' Daisy said, cutting Bex off before she could properly start speaking. 'And I need you to be honest, okay. I need to know if I'm turning this into a bigger deal than it is.'

Daisy heard Bex's intake of breath down the line. 'Is this about his parents? Do they hate you? Do you hate them?'

'Absolutely, but that's not what I need to tell you about.'

It was only as Daisy tried to steel herself that she realised her left hand was gripping the steering wheel so tightly that her knuckles were white. Obviously, she wasn't as okay with this whole thing as she'd tried to make out to Theo she was.

'I just found out that Theo also proposed to Heather,' she started.

She had decided to break the news into pieces. To see how Bex reacted to it bit by bit. Although it was hard to judge the slight hiss that she made down the line.

'And you didn't know about this?'

'Nope. It was a long time ago. Like, years before I came onto the scene. He says he didn't tell me because he completely forgot about it.'

'And do you believe him?'

'I don't know. I think so. I mean, he said she turned him down outright, and it was never discussed again. It was just something he did because he was feeling all paranoid about their relationship. But you'd think you'd remember proposing to someone, wouldn't you?'

Silence met Daisy's question and though she had removed her hand from the steering wheel and was flexing her fingers, she was struggling to remove all the tension from the rest of her body. What she needed was for Bex to reply and say it was all okay.

'I guess men think differently to us,' she said. 'And you trust

Theo, right? He clearly adores you. If it wasn't a big deal, then I think you need to take him at his word.'

Daisy nodded, despite the fact that Bex couldn't see. Silence swelled again, although this time it was broken by Claire's voice, calling in the distance.

'Bex, I think we are going to get busy again. And I want to speak to Daisy too. You can't take all the gossip, you know.'

'Sorry, Daisy, Claire needs me.'

'Sure, right. So you don't think it's a big deal.'

'I don't.'

'Great. Definitely not a big issue.'

'Definitely not.'

'Okay. And if he used the same ring for us both?'

'He did *what*?'

25

'I'm sorry. We'll be back in five minutes,' Claire said to a customer that Daisy couldn't see.

She and Bex had put the phone on video call and a chalk-board sign in the hatch for the coffee shop, saying they would be back soon. Now they were squished together on the sofa so Daisy could see them both as they talked.

'I'm sorry,' Claire said, needing Daisy to repeat everything again. 'So, he proposed to you with the same ring that he proposed to his former girlfriend, and you only found all this out because his mother – who we really do not like at all – told you this?'

'Pretty much,' Daisy said, feeling the weight sink into her stomach. 'But he insists he gave me the ring because it was a family heirloom. It was his grandmother's, and the pair of them were incredibly close. That's why he wanted me to have it. But he's said I can go and pick another if I want. Or he can choose another for me.'

'It better be a bloody expensive one,' Bex seethed. Any benefit of the doubt that she had previously offered Theo was gone, and now she was glaring at the phone. 'I can't believe he would do that.'

'I can,' Claire said.

'You can?' Daisy replied.

'Yes, this is Theo. It's like he said. That ring means a lot to him and so he wanted you to have it. Was it thoughtless? Yes. Did he mean to do it on purpose? No, of course he didn't. He adores you, Daisy. He even sent us photos of the ring to make sure we thought you'd like it.'

'He did?' Daisy said. 'When?'

'Months and months ago. Honestly, Heather was the furthest thing from his mind when he was looking at that. I promise, the only thing he was thinking about was you.'

This new piece of knowledge shifted a little of the tension that had fixed around Daisy's neck and shoulders. In her imagination, Theo had simply dug in the back of his drawers to find the ring he had used once to propose before. But if he had sent photos to Bex and Claire, that obviously wasn't the case.

'Bex, what do you think?' Daisy said. Having one friend sitting on either side of the fence wasn't particularly helpful. For a moment, she thought Bex was going to stick to her guns and say that Daisy needed to ditch Theo then and there, but she shook her head and let out a long groan.

'You see, this is why I'm single. Because even the good guys go and do bloody stupid things like this. I just don't have the patience for it.'

There was no denying that Bex's impossibly high standards played a part in her ending relationships before they ever got too serious. But right now, no matter how selfish it was, Daisy didn't want to focus on her friend. She needed their help.

'But you think I'm correct in forgiving him, right?' Daisy said, needing Bex to give her a clear answer.

'I do. But… if he makes one more mistake, he's out.'

Daisy laughed. The way Bex spoke made it sound like it was she who was in a relationship, but in a way, it was. Daisy's friendships meant more to her than anyone, and she didn't know how she would cope if they somehow became divided.

'Where is he?' Claire said, suddenly drawing Daisy's attention to the fact that Theo had now been gone for over twenty minutes. It was certainly a lot longer than the minute he'd promised. She was about to say as much when he appeared in the doorway. Or rather, his legs appeared. The top half of his body was entirely obscured by various black bags and boxes that he was carrying.

'I better go,' Daisy said, feeling a need to get out there and help him before he dropped something. 'But I'll speak to you later, okay?'

'Speak later. Love you loads.'

'Love you too.'

A minute later, Daisy had hung up the phone, climbed out of the car and was rushing towards Theo.

'What the hell is all this?' she said, as she took one of the large bags from him, revealing his face and a large smile behind it.

'Who needs a hotel,' he said, 'when we've got a tent?'

26

'You want to go camping?' Daisy said as she put one of the bags down on the ground. Now that she looked more clearly at the assortment Theo carried, there was obviously camping gear in there, like the small sacks for sleeping bags and another which jangled insistently and was probably filled with poles for the tents.

'I have a buddy that owns a campsite down by one of the lakes. It's beautiful at this time of year. His parents used to run it, and we would spend all our summers there when we were kids. He took over it a couple of years ago and I'd been hoping to take you to see it at some point, but I didn't think we'd have enough time to go during this trip. This is working out perfectly.'

His face was beaming, and Daisy could see the small child he had been, playing in the water, living life to the fullest. She held on to the image for a second, only for another person to flick into her mind. A young Heather, perfectly dressed even as a pre-teen, playing with Theo as they splashed around together. With a sharp intake of breath, Daisy shook the thought from her head and smiled.

'Well, then I guess that seems perfect. Have you told your parents?'

For the first time, Theo's smile faltered, then dropped altogether as he gritted his teeth.

'Yes,' he said. 'I did.'

Daisy waited for him to expand and say a little more. Perhaps how they didn't want them to leave, or how Penelope was sorry for making Daisy feel so uncomfortable, and yet Theo remained absolutely silent, so Daisy pressed again.

'And what did they say?'

'Honestly?' he spoke through a hiss. 'You're probably better off not knowing.'

The words churned in Daisy's stomach. So no apology then. It was clear that whatever they had said had been enough to upset Theo, although Daisy suspected that any harsh comments were probably directed at her. Was she being too sensitive? That sounded like a line Ice Queen Penelope would have used. Wanting people to be decent wasn't overly sensitive in Daisy's book. It was just called being nice.

Trying to shake Penelope to the same place in her mind that she had just banished Heather, Daisy looked up at Theo and smiled.

'Well, I'm sorry if what they said was upsetting, but they are not the priority of this weekend. You and I are. And I think camping sounds perfect.'

One of the things Daisy loved about her and Theo's relationship was how he always seemed to know the right thing to say when she was struggling, and when Theo's face lit up, she knew she had managed it for him, too. His eyes twinkled as his smile broadened.

'You're right, it is,' he said. 'You and I will always be the priority. Now, let's go camping.'

27

The first stop was to a nearby supermarket to stock up on provisions, though Daisy didn't go into the shop with Theo. Instead, she used the opportunity to text Bex and Claire and keep them up to date on progress, mainly that they were abandoning the parents' house and going camping and that she was going to believe Theo when he said it was all a simple mistake not telling her about the proposal to Heather. As for the ring, she wasn't exactly sure where she stood on that one. She knew it had sentimental meaning for Theo, but it was still hard not to look at it and see him proposing to Heather too. Though maybe, she hoped, those feelings would change with time.

After taking almost as long in the shop as he had collecting the camping gear, Theo appeared at the car, laden with bags.

'I thought we were only camping for one night?' Daisy questioned as she watched him pile all the things into the backseat.

'We are, but we're camping in luxury. I borrowed Dad's old portable barbeque, but I needed to get some coals for it. Just because we're sleeping outside doesn't mean we can't dine well.'

According to Theo, the camping ground was about a thirty-minute drive away, which seemed a fair distance, considering how he had mentioned that this was someone he had grown up with.

'We met at boarding school,' Theo explained. This part of his past Daisy did know about. Just like she knew he had only gone there for a couple of years.

'He's pretty much the only person who I still keep in touch with. We shared a dorm my first term there and my last. It's funny, you know, he always said that as soon as he could, he would get out of the Lake District. Make something of himself. He always insisted that the last thing he wanted to do was run his parents' place.'

'So what happened?' Daisy asked.

'I don't know. He went and worked in London for a couple of years, and even did a stint working in Asia, but I guess this place draws a lot of people back in the end.'

When he finished speaking, Daisy turned her head and gazed out of the window. The long summer nights meant the sun was far from setting, but a dusky, muted light was reflecting off the hills and trees, creating a shimmering, almost ethereal look. Yes, she could see that growing up in a place like this would call back to you. The thought caused a knot to tighten in her stomach.

'What about you?' she asked.

'What about me?' Theo replied.

'Does it draw you back? Have you always thought you'd end up back here in the end?'

Rather than replying immediately, Theo continued to gaze out of the window, his brow furrowing just a fraction.

'I don't know. Honestly, I don't. When I left, I hadn't planned on it being forever, but apart from the scenery, I guess I don't have much to come back for. Most of my close friends have moved on, my sister's settled up in Scotland with no intention of ever moving back, and as for my parents... Well, I guess you understand why I tend not to visit that often now. Although to be fair, today they were pretty vile. From what I gathered, Dad spent all day yesterday playing golf and Mum was pissed off at him. Still, that doesn't excuse her behaviour at all.'

No, it didn't, Daisy thought. It wasn't as if Daisy hadn't had issues with her own mother over the years. Behaviour like the previous night, when Pippa had drunkenly insulted someone's pastries, were getting increasingly common and then there was the entire thing about hiding her past and the truth about Daisy's father until it was too late for them to make amends. But then her mother did amazing things for Daisy, too. Like finishing the trip to Slimbridge with her, and finally giving her all of Johnny's old paintings. If her mother had been like Penelope, she suspected she would have left as soon as she was able to live on her own and possibly never come back, but she also knew that that was far easier said than done. It didn't matter how mad they drove you, family was family. She knew that.

As she daydreamed, Theo reached across and took her hand.

'All I know is that my home now is wherever you are,' he said, taking his eyes momentarily off the road so that he could flash her a smile. 'And I don't care if that is on a narrowboat in the Essex countryside, or a tent in the middle of the Lake District. It's you and me, Daisy May.'

Daisy was about to respond, a smile forming on her lips, when a large signpost came into view on the side of the road and Theo flicked on the indicators. Slowing down, he readied to take the turn.

'This is us,' he said.

28

When Theo had said 'camping,' Daisy had envisioned rough pathways and a trek into the middle of nowhere, perhaps to a near-empty field with a dodgy-looking toilet and shower block, or a place to put a disposable barbeque, but what she was seeing was a long way from the rustic image she had imagined. As they drove down the newly tarmacked road, they were led by various signposts, pointing out everything from the children's playground to the boat hire and the park shop. There were also several signs pointing to glamping tepees and shepherds' huts.

'Wow, it's changed. They've done this up a lot since I was last here,' Theo said, almost as if he were speaking to himself. 'When we used to come, there were two toilet blocks and a couple of tire swings. I knew Liam had spent a fair bit doing it up, but I had no idea he'd put so much work into it. This looks good. Really good.'

The speed they were driving at reminded Daisy of the *September Rose*. On the canal, a top speed of four miles an hour was considered entirely reasonable, and it didn't feel like they were going any faster than that. Countless signs were posted around, declaring the slow speed limit, while also displaying warnings such as 'Ducks Crossing' and 'Beware Children'. Not that Daisy needed to see a sign for that one – it was pretty obvious. On every side of the road, children were running around and playing. Some were dressed in wetsuits and life jackets as if they had just come back from a trip out on the water, while others were riding their bikes or skipping.

'It's busy,' Daisy said, stating the obvious.

'Right?' Theo replied. 'Liam said it was pretty packed, but he assured me there was a free camping spot. I wrote the number on my phone. It's forty-something, I think.'

Daisy continued to stare out of the window, trying to take it all in.

'There's a sign up here for the car park,' she said. 'I think we probably have to park up there and walk the rest of the way to the campsite.'

'Sounds good,' Theo said. 'Although I hope it's not too far. I'm starting to regret buying all that shopping.'

* * *

There were both positives and negatives to the plot Liam had designated for them. The main positive was that it looked directly out over the lake, with an unobstructed view of the water. When they finally arrived at their designated patch of land, Daisy stopped in her tracks, her breath stolen by the view.

'This is stunning,' she said.

The sun was on its downward descent and had coloured the clouds deep shades of fuchsia and magenta, which were reflected in the perfectly still water. Her fingers itched as she stared out at the vista. It was idyllic. Incredible. Exactly the type of place that she would love to paint.

'Why don't you stay here, and I'll go back and get the rest of the stuff,' Theo said. His voice drew Daisy away from her daydream, and at the same time reminded her of the one negative part of their plot: it was about as far from the car park as they could get, and they simply hadn't managed to carry all of their gear in one go.

'No,' Daisy said, shaking her head in response. 'That doesn't make any sense. I don't know how to set up this tent of yours, and you want to do the cooking. It makes far more sense for you to stay here and set everything up, and I'll go back to the car and fetch anything we've left.'

'Are you sure?' Theo said.

'Of course I am.'

'I don't mind walking with you.'

Daisy reached up on her tiptoes and kissed him softly on his lips.

'I might be an engaged woman, but I can still manage to walk to a car and carry a few groceries by myself.'

'Okay, but if you need help, you only have to call me.'

With a playful sigh, she gave him one more quick peck before turning around and walking back to the car.

29

This wasn't the first time Daisy had gone camping, but it was a very different experience to the camping holidays she had been on with her mother as a child. Then they had gone to the type of resorts where they already had the tents set up and she spent five hours a day at the kids' club, while Pippa slept in and drank wine at lunchtime. It wasn't always camping in tents, either. Some-times, they stayed in mobile homes, or chalets, but the kids' club and wine were always a common feature. Daisy didn't think badly of her mother for that, though. Even from a young age, she'd understood that, as a single parent who worked full-time and a bit, her mother needed any chance of respite she could get. And as an only child, Daisy had enjoyed the opportunity to make new friends who she'd play with all day. But it would have been nice to have had a few more memories of her childhood that involved adventures with her mum. Like she suspected these children were getting, as they walked back to their tents with paddle-boards on their shoulders and parents laughing beside them.

A slight sense of melancholy shrouded Daisy's thoughts, but she shrugged it away. She couldn't regret any part of her childhood. Her mother had done what she'd thought was best and Daisy wouldn't have grown into the person she was now without it. A person she was incredibly proud to be. Besides, they had probably made up for any missed adventures when her mum came and completed the last part of the journey from Wildflower Lock to Slimbridge. That trip felt like a year's worth of holidays crammed into less than two weeks.

Despite the generous signposting around the park, Daisy's lack of concentration, and desire to take in everything around her, meant that after five minutes of walking, there was no sign of the car park. Instead, she had found herself in a very different area of the campsite.

Great fire pits were set up in front of cloth tepees, many of which were opened to display the various cushions and blankets laid out inside. There were large wooden swing seats, again adorned with plush blankets, and various little gazebos dotted around the space. It appeared like several families had come together in a large group, and as the children played, the adults had set up a speaker that was blasting music into the air.

'Wow,' Daisy said, as she noticed that one of the parents had turned a gazebo into a makeshift bar and was busy shaking cocktails as they laughed with their friends. She had thought a couple of times about whether or not she should try to get a licence for selling alcohol on the *September Rose*. There was definitely a market for it, at least in the summer as people wanted to cool off and quench their thirst with a crisp cider or a chilled white wine, but it was a whole heap of hoops to jump through and she wasn't sure if she wanted the added pressure. But as she watched the families enjoying this time together, she considered the idea yet again.

After a couple of minutes, Daisy realised she had been staring for far longer than was probably appropriate and she needed to head to the car and get back to the campsite before Theo started wondering where she had got to. And so this time, when she moved off, she made a far more concerted effort to follow the signposts.

Given how out of her way she had walked, Daisy passed two sets of shower blocks, along with a kayak hire and the launderette, before she finally reached the car park, and was about to click the button to unlock the boot of the car when a voice called out to her.

'Daisy?'

Stopping in her tracks, she turned around, frowning, wondering why she recognised the voice. The minute she laid eyes on the person, she knew exactly why.

Daisy's stomach dropped as her jaw fell slack at the pristine image in front of her. Of all the people she didn't want to see right now.

'Heather?'

30

Daisy was gawping. She knew she was, though in her defence, there were several reasons. First, she had spent the entire time since leaving Theo's parents' house trying not to think of this particular woman, and now found herself face-to-face with her. It was as if her worst fears had manifested. The perfect daughter-in-law, the woman Theo should have married, was there, standing in the car park only feet away from her. But that wasn't the only reason Daisy was staring, because along with Heather's perfectly curled loose ringlets, impeccable make-up and faultless taste in clothes, she was sporting something Daisy had never seen her wearing before: a very large baby bump.

'Heather,' Daisy said again. Apparently, the ex's name was the only word she could manage.

'Yup, it's me.'

When Daisy finally drew her eyes away from Heather's belly, her line of sight only moved slightly to her left hand, where two gold rings were sparkling in the evening light, one of which had a huge diamond in the centre.

As the silence stretched between them, Heather let out a light chuckle, breaking the tension that was even more pronounced than during tea with Theo's parents.

'It's fair to say that quite a lot has changed since you and I last saw each other,' Heather said. 'I guess that if you're here, it means that you and Theo are still going strong?'

Daisy wasn't sure why her eyes immediately flicked down to her own left hand as Heather said this. Why her attention locked on Theo's grandmother's ring. Perhaps it was just a reaction to seeing Heather's own ring, or maybe because she wasn't sure how Heather would react at seeing it on Daisy's finger. Still, there was no way she could hide it, and the minute she looked down, Daisy knew Heather's line of sight followed.

'Wow, so things are still going well,' Heather said, her eyes widening at the gem. 'Congratulations.'

'And you too, of course, for the baby. And the marriage. And, yes, congratulations.' Daisy could hear herself stuttering away and was pretty sure she sounded incomprehensible. But what else was she meant to say? Congratulations was the right thing, wasn't it? Yes, she was sure it was, which was why she carried on. 'It's brilliant news. Wonderful. Absolutely fantastic.' She wasn't sure how she was going to stop or if she even could when, without warning, Heather stepped forward and wrapped her arms tightly around her in a hug. Well, as tight as the bump would allow. When she stepped back, her face was beaming.

'I really am so happy for you guys,' Heather said. 'I know it was a little weird there for a while, when Theo and I were still clinging on, trying to make things work, but thank goodness they didn't.'

'Yes, yes,' Daisy said, not sure why the words were sticking to the back of her throat all of a sudden. Another silence started to swell and Daisy had a sudden sinking feeling that perhaps Heather was going to invite them to join her for a drink.

'So we are staying in the yurts—' Heather began, almost certainly confirming Daisy's fears. So before she could say any more, Daisy cut across her.

'Well, I should get our things from the car. We are only staying one night and Theo's already cooking. I don't want him to worry that I've fallen into the lake or something.'

Daisy chuckled, but unlike Heather's light laughter, which sounded almost ethereal in its breathy effortlessness, Daisy sounded more like a chicken who had got its neck caught in a fence.

Still, Heather's soft smile was nothing but polite. 'Of course. Absolutely. Perhaps I'll see you around.'

'Yes, yes, of course.'

'And don't forget to send Theo my love.'

'Right. Your love. Of course,' Daisy said, then before Heather could say anything else, Daisy turned around and was practically sprinting the last few feet back to the car.

31

Daisy didn't have to tell Theo she had bumped into Heather, she decided as she walked back to the camping plot with her arms laden with bags. She could just pretend she had got lost and say that was why it had taken her so long to get back to the car. It would be true, after all. Or partly true. It wasn't like she had spent anywhere near as long talking to Heather as she had wandering aimlessly around, looking at all the scenery. And it wouldn't be as if he could judge her for staying silent on the matter. Starting a conversation about Heather when Daisy had been doing everything she could to forget about her was the last thing she wanted to do. And it wasn't like she expected Heather to come wandering over to their side of the campsite, where people pitched up their little tents on small patches of grass. Not when she was staying in the luxury yurts.

Daisy thought through the practicalities of keeping the encounter a secret. They could turn in early for the night, then wake up early and head back to the hotel. Even if they couldn't check in until later, it would be perfectly possible to avoid her.

But... Daisy knew the counterargument was going to win

before she even tried to convince herself. No matter how much she wished otherwise, she couldn't keep this from Theo. For starters, there was the fact that Heather might seek Theo out, and if she did, it would certainly come out that she and Daisy had shared an earlier conversation and Daisy would be left trying to explain why she hadn't said anything without making herself sound like a jealous, paranoid girlfriend. Then there was the fact that the last thing she wanted to do was start keeping things from her fiancé only twenty-four hours into their engagement. That seemed like a disaster waiting to happen. There was also a third reason that Daisy couldn't keep seeing Heather from Theo. One she wasn't aware of until she arrived back at their plot, where the tent was already up and large, orange flames were billowing on the fire.

'Hey,' she said, as she opened the tent and prepared to put the bags inside. Only before she could move that far, Theo was on his feet. With his hands around his waist, he smiled broadly, but only momentarily, before his expression dropped and his eyes narrowed on her.

'What happened?' he said. 'You look like you've seen a ghost.'

Daisy released an internal sigh that was somewhere between relief and disappointment. She should have known Theo would spot something was wrong with her straight away.

'A ghost,' she said with a groan. 'That's one way of putting it.'

32

Daisy took in a deep breath. Theo was staring at her, his eyes filled with concern, but her throat had done that same clogged-up thing it did earlier when Heather tried to speak to her.

'Daisy, what do you mean you saw a ghost?' Theo said. 'Why were you so long? What happened?'

She could see his worry intensifying. With another deep breath in, Daisy forced her mouth into a smile.

'Not a ghost, no,' she said. 'Just an ex.'

'An ex? Who? Your ex?' Daisy shook her head and Theo's brow furrowed for an instant before the realisation dawned. 'Heather? She's here?'

'Over in the luxury yurts,' Daisy said. As much as she didn't want to recall the situation, all the tension she had felt on the way back over about whether she should tell Theo was gone. That wasn't to say she felt at ease.

'You saw her? You spoke to her?'

Daisy nodded. 'In the car park. I got lost and ended up at the yurts. I think she might have seen me there and followed me over to say hello.'

Theo's expression was pinched as he blew out a long breath with a slow hiss.

'Oh, wow. Well, was everything okay? How was she?' He tried to sound casual, but Daisy knew him better than that.

'Oh, she was great. I mean, she looked great. Very happy,' Daisy said, recalling the way Heather had beamed so brightly, she was practically luminous. 'Oh, and married.'

'Married?'

'Yes, at least she had the rings. So I guess so.'

'Wow. Right.'

Theo's jaw was hanging lower and lower with every piece of information Daisy told him. And she still hadn't shared the biggest piece of news, but she knew there was no point in keeping it hidden.

'She was pregnant too.'

'Pregnant?' At this, Theo's eyebrows rose so high, they almost reached his hairline. Dropping his hands from Daisy's side, he offered a short shake of his head. 'Wow, well, I'm sorry I wasn't there to talk to her with you. That's brilliant news. Absolutely fantastic.'

'It is?'

'That she's married and pregnant. Of course it is! I mean, she always wanted kids, and she has a smart head on her shoulders and is a damn good judge of character. There's no chance she would have married someone if she didn't think he was something special.'

His smile broadened, causing a light to glimmer in his eyes. 'This is such fantastic news. I'm so happy for her. Really happy. She's in the yurts, you say?'

'Yes, it's all the way over on the other side of the campsite,' Daisy replied.

She had suspected Theo had made the comment because he,

too, was worried about them bumping into her. But the next thing he said erased any such hope.

'Well, we should go and say congratulations,' he said. 'It looks like it's good news all around at the moment.'

33

Daisy didn't want to go and say congratulations to Theo's ex. She hadn't wanted to see her in the first place. She didn't want to be in the same campsite as her, or, if possible, the same country. And yet, Theo's eyes continued to glimmer away. There was no denying he was truly happy Heather was there. Daisy didn't know why it surprised her. He was the type of person who didn't bear grudges, and any issues about how their relationship ended were to do with him and Daisy, not Heather. But still, that didn't change the fact that Daisy didn't want to see her. In fact, after the day she'd had, she didn't want to see anyone at all, other than Theo.

'You've just lit the barbecue,' Daisy said as she glanced around her, finding a viable excuse why they couldn't go. 'We can't leave it unattended, not with children running about everywhere. It would be a hazard.'

'Oh, yes, of course, you're right.' Theo's face altered slightly. It wasn't like it fell completely, it just flickered a little, and Daisy could see the disappointment that he tried not to show. Guilt bloomed in her chest. Shouldn't she feel grateful that she had such a lovely fiancé, he still wanted to maintain a friendly relationship with his ex? And it wasn't like she was jealous of Heather, or worried that Theo would suddenly start regretting the decision not to stay with her. Heather was obviously very settled in her new situation. So why was it a problem if he wanted to go and catch up?

Drawing in a deep breath, Daisy pushed her insecurities as far down as she could before she spoke.

'You know what, why don't you go, and I'll stay here with the barbecue,' she said, forcing her cheeks into a smile as she tried to sound as casual as possible. 'That makes the most sense.'

Once again, Theo's expression shifted. His eyes narrowed slightly.

'You're sure? No, don't be silly. I can't leave you here. We came up to have a romantic weekend away.'

'Yes, but we were going to be spending the first night of that with your parents anyway. Honestly, I don't mind. Besides, I've been wanting to get a few sketches of the landscape down since we first turned up here. This way, I don't have to worry about you disturbing me.' She flashed a smile as she finished speaking, just so he knew she was joking.

'You are amazing, you know that?' Theo said as he wrapped a hand around her waist and pulled her into him. 'I don't know what I did to deserve someone as amazing as you.'

'I don't think that's true,' Daisy said. 'I mean, you started by doing all the carpentry on my boat. That was definitely a good place to start.'

Theo let out a deep laugh as he stared into Daisy's eyes. It was the type of laugh that set her stomach into butterflies and left her thinking exactly the same thing – how did she get so lucky? Of course, it didn't matter if Theo wanted to see his ex. It wasn't like it was going to become a regular thing.

As if reading her thoughts, Theo stepped away from her and brushed a strand of hair behind her ear.

'Heather's over in the yurts, you say?' he asked.

Daisy nodded. 'Yes, they're over on the luxury side of the campsite.'

'Great, well, I'll head over there now. It'll give you some peace so you can get a couple of sketches done, and by the time I come back, the coals should have cooled enough for me to get on with the cooking.'

After one more long and slightly lingering kiss, Theo dropped Daisy's hands, turned around, and headed off in the direction that Daisy had come from. Back towards Heather.

34

For a moment, Daisy simply stood there watching as Theo strode off to the other side of the campsite. Off towards Heather. Only once he was out of sight did she turn back to look at the lake. The clouds had grown denser since they had arrived, and muted the light of the setting sun, yet it was no less beautiful than it had been before. Each breath of air felt cleaner than the previous. Whether it was because of the altitude or the lake water or the lack of narrowboats, Daisy didn't know, but it was undeniably different to the air she had grown used to at Wildflower Lock. And whatever the reason, she knew it would be impossible to capture in her paintings the way she really wanted to.

With her mind flickering away from painting, she glanced down at her finger to look at the ring. It really was stunning, but now, even more than ever, she was seeing Heather in it. She couldn't help but imagine what it would have been like if it was this ring on Heather's finger, rather than the large solitaire she had just seen. Was that really how she wanted to start her engagement? Feeling the shadow of Theo's ex everywhere they went?

'You're not doing this, Daisy,' she said to herself as she felt her mood slipping. She was in a beautiful place and she was going to make the most of it.

Pushing her shoulders back and determined to remain positive about the situation, she turned back towards the tent, ready to grab her sketch pad and start doodling away, when her phone started ringing.

Daisy groaned. It was lovely that the girls wanted to make sure she was doing okay, but she had spoken to them when Theo was in the supermarket and she really didn't feel like filling them in on the latest development. Her plan was to switch the phone to silent and let it ring out. Only when she glanced at the screen, it wasn't Bex or Claire's name flashing boldly. It was Mum. For a second, Daisy considered sticking with her original plan and switching the phone to silent, reasoning that she could always send a message in five minutes or so saying she was in the shower. But no sooner had the thought crossed her mind than she dismissed it. Her mum would want an update on how everything had gone sooner or later, and would likely keep ringing until she got one. Especially if she'd had a drink. There was no point delaying the inevitable.

'Hey, Mum,' Daisy said, adding an extra layer of cheeriness to her voice. 'How are you?'

'Hey, love. I didn't ring to tell you about myself. Now come on, how's the trip going? Let me guess, Theo's parents are as madly in love with you as we all are.'

Daisy lifted her eyes to the sky and the swathes of white clouds as she drew in a long breath.

'It's been interesting,' she said, the idea of painting now completely abandoned.

35

The good news was that by the time Daisy finished the conversation with her mum, she was feeling slightly better, but that was mainly because she'd felt like she had to put a positive spin on everything.

There was a time in her life when she would have told her mother the absolute truth, no matter what, but it became difficult to maintain such a practice when she learned her mum had been lying to her for most of her life. They still spoke regularly, of course, and still had a relationship far better than a lot of mothers and daughters she knew, but it was changed. Different from what it had been only three or four years before. Now she felt the need to keep herself slightly distant from her mum. Emotionally, at least. Especially when she could already tell her mother had had a drink. The last thing Daisy wanted was everyone in Wildflower Lock knowing her business, and Daisy suspected that if she said anything too negative, Pippa wouldn't manage to keep it to herself.

'There's a reason Theo moved away from his parents,' Daisy said, parroting what Theo had said to her. 'Honestly, they just weren't particularly nice. And after a few snide comments, we decided we didn't want to spend the night in the house with them, so we've come out camping instead, and it's absolutely beautiful.'

'What do you mean, snide comments?' her mother said, latching on to the part of the comment Daisy had hoped she would skip over.

'Well, I guess it's because they haven't met me. I'm sure you'd be a bit funny if I told you I was marrying someone you had never even met.'

Pippa huffed down the line. 'They could have come down and visited you two.'

'Yes, they could,' Daisy said, wishing there was a way she could steer the conversation in a different direction, although before she had considered how, her mother was already on a different topic.

'So what's this campsite like? I take it there are lots of hills? And lakes too? Switch the video on so I can see it.'

Following her mother's instructions, Daisy flicked to a video call and promptly swivelled the camera around so it faced the lake.

'Look at that,' her mum said with an exaggerated sigh. 'Nicholas, come and look at this. It's stunning. Look at the size of those hills.'

'They might actually be mountains,' Daisy said. 'I probably need to check that with Theo. But yes, it's very pretty.'

'Where is Theo?' Pippa asked, once again picking up on a tiny part of Daisy's comment that she wished she'd not said. 'I should probably say hello to my future son-in-law. Where is he? Get him to come and say hello.'

Daisy's stomach plummeted. There was no chance she was going to tell her mother where Theo had actually gone. Given

Pippa's track record with relationships, there was no way she would believe anyone – even Theo – just wanted to say congratulations to an ex without some ulterior motive. And so Daisy was preparing a lie about him using the campsite bathroom when she suddenly saw him in the distance.

'He's just there,' she said, turning the camera around so her mother could see him. 'He's just been for a bit of a walk.'

'And you didn't want to go with him?'

Daisy swallowed, annoyed that such a nonchalant remark had left her needing to find another lie to follow it.

'I was keeping an eye on the barbecue. Actually, Mum, I should probably get going. I told him that I'd have something ready before he got back, but we've just been chatting away.'

'Of course, love. I don't want to interrupt this time for you. But think about what his parents said, okay? They know him best, after all.'

For a second, Daisy was sure she must have misheard her mother and that she must have said *don't think* about what his parents said. But before she could question it, her mum had hung up and Theo was standing right next to her.

'Hey, was that your mum or the girls?' he said, planting a kiss on her cheek.

'Mum,' Daisy replied.

'Well, I'm sorry I didn't get to say hi. We were chatting a bit longer than I thought.'

Given how long Daisy had been lost in conversation with her mother, she hadn't been keeping track of time particularly, but she was surprised when she glanced down at her phone and saw that he had been gone for almost an hour.

'It's not a problem,' Daisy said. 'But I am getting hungry.'

'Then I shall put food on now,' Theo said, moving towards the barbecue.

As he sorted out their meal for the night, Daisy considered whether she wanted to ask him her next question. She really didn't want their entire trip to be dominated by conversation about Heather, but at the same time knew it would be churlish not to say anything. So, as nonchalantly as she could, she said, 'How was Heather?'

Theo's smile gleamed. 'She was incredible. She's having twins. Can you believe it? We always talked about twins because she'd always wanted to have them. How lucky is that?'

Daisy felt a lump forming in her throat, but it took her a minute to work out why.

'Super lucky,' she said, before turning around and facing the tent so Theo couldn't see her expression.

36

It didn't matter how much she tried to ignore it. The lump in Daisy's throat was going nowhere.

Even when the food had cooked and they were sitting outside, eating, it was there, stopping her from enjoying her meal.

'Is everything all right?' Theo asked. 'You've been a bit quiet. Is it Mum and Dad still? Or was it me going to see Heather? Honestly, she was really pleased about our engagement. Genuinely. I couldn't have imagined it two years ago, but I guess once she met the right person, she got it. When you know, you know, right?'

Daisy nodded, grateful that she could use chewing food as a reason not to offer a proper answer. She wouldn't say she knew straight away with Theo, and neither did he. Not at their first meeting, at least. Sure, this relationship was very different from the one she'd had with Paul. But that was probably because she was older, too. More mature.

'You and Heather talked about having children, then?' she said, finally voicing the thought that had been niggling at her since Theo returned. 'You knew she wanted twins.'

'She always said she wanted twins; she didn't want to have to spend years of her life lost to sleepless nights by having one after another,' Theo explained. 'I'll be honest, the idea of it terrified me. I have a pair of cousins who are twins, and I remember all the horror stories my aunt would tell me about how the minute she got one to sleep, the other would wake up, and she could never remember which one she had fed and which she hadn't. She was pretty sure she didn't sleep for three years. I don't think I could deal with that. But Heather insisted it would be easiest in the long run. I guess now she'll find out.'

Daisy was only half listening. He had seemed to miss the point. It wasn't that Heather wanted twins that had out her out of sorts; it was the fact that Heather and Theo had obviously talked about having children, and not just in a passing comment way. She couldn't remember when, or even if, the comment had ever arisen between the two of them and if it had, there had certainly never been enough detail to decide how many or how far apart they would want them.

'So you definitely want children?' Daisy said, feeling the need to voice the question.

'Of course. Don't you?'

'I don't know.'

'You don't know?' Theo's brow furrowed deeply, and two long creases formed between his eyebrows. 'I always assumed you'd want at least one.'

'Why would you assume that?' Daisy asked. She didn't want to sound so sharp, but the more she thought about it, the more certain she was that they hadn't ever discussed it, and yet Theo obviously had some very clear assumptions about what she would and wouldn't want in the future.

'Well, there's the way you're so close to Amelia, to start with,'

Theo said. 'And you're always so good with the kids who come to the coffee shop.'

'It's a bit different, smiling at a baby when you hand their mum a cappuccino, as opposed to having your own that you're stuck with twenty-four seven.'

'*Stuck with*?' Theo said. 'So I take it you don't want children?'

'I didn't say that.'

'I don't think people who want children consider themselves as being *stuck with* them. Most people actually like their company.'

Daisy could feel a sense of ire rising inside her, and not just because of the assumption Theo had made. She had met plenty of mums when she had been working in London who very much felt stuck with their children. It wasn't a long-term feeling, and it didn't mean they didn't love them, but she would need several more hands than her own to count the number who had found a sense of relief in coming back to work and having some adult company, even if it was just for one day a week.

'I think parenting is a bit more nuanced than either wanting to be with your children every single second of the day, or not wanting to be with them at all,' she said, trying to add a reasoned argument to her point. 'I think staying at home works really well for people like Claire who are great at all those arts and crafts and homebody activities, but I think it's a lot more complicated when you have a career or a business to think of.'

'You mean like you have a business to think of?'

'Yes.'

'So you're saying you don't want children because they would interfere with your business?'

'Will you stop putting words into my mouth?' Daisy couldn't remember the last time she had shouted at Theo, or if she ever had. But the words left her mouth in the closest thing to a yell she had ever done. 'I didn't say that. I didn't say I didn't want children. I said I hadn't thought about it properly, and to be honest, I think that type of thing requires a lot of thought. It is a lifetime commitment, after all.'

At this, Theo tilted his head to the side. 'And you're saying that Heather didn't think about it properly?'

'What? Why are we talking about Heather now?' Daisy's jaw was hanging open. 'I was talking about us, because it feels like we haven't done that enough.'

Theo was shaking his head, as if Daisy was the one being unreasonable.

'I don't understand where this has come from,' he said.

'No, that's clear.' Despite her plate still being half full, Daisy slammed it down on the ground beside her and stood up. Theo had spent a great deal of time marinating the meat and creating a salad to go with it, but she didn't care. She wasn't hungry any more.

'I'm going for a walk,' she said, picking up her phone from the ground.

'But it's going to be dark soon,' Theo protested, looking as if he were about to stand up after her.

'Then I guess I'll walk in the dark.'

37

Every part of Daisy's body was pounding with anger as she marched away. She didn't look back. Somehow, she knew Theo would have the sense not to follow her this time.

It was his gall to put words in her mouth that really got to her. The way he had said she wouldn't have children because of the business. He was implying she was selfish. That was what he was doing. And then to bring up Heather at a point in a conversation where tensions were already so high. It was like he was after a fight.

Another thought tugged in Daisy's chest. Maybe that was exactly what he had been after. Maybe he had seen Heather, decided he'd made a mistake, and come back hoping to bait and goad and upset Daisy so much that she was the one who ended things. Well, he'd been sorely mistaken. If he wanted to break off this engagement – or whatever the hell it was they were going through – then he would have to look her in the eye as he did it.

Daisy's pace didn't slow. If anything, it got quicker. She needed to put space between them, and that was exactly what she intended to do. Several minutes after storming off, she reached a narrow track labelled as a public footpath that led off the caravan park's land. As she finally began to slow, the last time they'd had a big argument resurfaced in her mind. It had been when Theo had discovered that she'd been secretly seeing him and Christian at the same time. She hadn't meant to end up in such a sticky situation, having been desperate to find a way out of it, but she'd not wanted to hurt either of them. In the end, though, the way Theo had found out had been particularly cruel, given that Christian had kissed Daisy in front of dozens of people at the charity auction. But Daisy had owned up to her mess and taken full responsibility for how badly everything had gone. This time, however, there was no chance she was going to go back with a grovelling apology. She was not the one in the wrong.

Daisy didn't know where she was walking. All she knew was that she wouldn't stop until she had calmed down, and at this rate, she would be halfway back to the Cotswolds before that happened.

Still steaming with fury, she looked along the track a little way ahead and spotted a building that looked remarkably like a pub. With a new purpose to her walk, she picked up the pace. She didn't care how many bottles of wine were sitting in carrier bags in the tent. Drinking them would mean going back to Theo, and that wasn't something she wanted to do.

38

Daisy stepped into the building and glanced around her. The space was separated into two distinct areas: the bar, which stretched out in a narrow room towards her right in which a couple of people were sitting on stools sipping on drinks, and the restaurant part, which arced around to her left and, from what she could tell, was completely packed. It was a far classier establishment than she had expected from outside.

'Have you got a booking?' A woman dressed entirely in black and holding a tablet appeared from nowhere as Daisy loitered in the doorway.

'Uh, no,' Daisy said.

'Well, I'm afraid we're fully booked. Unless you want to wait for half an hour? Is it a table for two?'

'I actually just wanted a drink,' Daisy said, gesturing to the bar to her right, at which point, the woman crinkled her nose.

'Oh, right? The bar entrance is at the other end, but no worries. Take a seat wherever you like up there.'

With that, the woman turned around and scurried back to the restaurant.

With her pace substantially slower than it had been, Daisy moved over to the bar. There were over half a dozen barstools along the length of the marble counter, though only two were occupied. Still, she took one at the farthest end, as far away from the other patrons as she could and had barely taken her seat when the barman appeared on the other side.

'What can I get you?' he said.

'A large glass of your house white,' Daisy replied instantly. 'A *very* large glass.'

He tilted his head to the side and eyed her with curiosity. 'Well, two of our large glasses only cost five pounds less than the entire bottle, if you'd rather go down that route.'

'Are you encouraging me to drink an entire bottle of wine by myself?' Daisy said, gesturing to the sign at the side of the bar that said:

We encourage responsible drinking only and have the right to refuse service.

The barman snorted a brief chuckle of laughter.

'No, I was just trying to save you a bit of money, that's all. You've got the face of someone who looks like they plan on staying here a while.'

'Is that right?' Daisy said.

'Perhaps the face of someone that's got a man on her mind? Or maybe a woman.'

Daisy felt her breath quivering as she held the air in her lungs. Part of her wanted to tell the barman to go and shove his pop psychology and get her the glass of wine she had asked for. But at the same time, he had been spot on. It would probably take her at least two glasses before she felt anywhere near ready enough to deal with Theo. So with a long sigh and not a hint of a smile on her face, she said, 'Fine, then. Make it a bottle.'

39

Daisy was sitting on the barstool with a topped-up glass of wine and the rest of the bottle in an ice bucket. For a minute, she just stared at the drink, holding the stem between her fingers. She had no idea where she was. That was the truth of the situation. She had walked in pretty much a straight line from the campsite to reach the pub, but any further than that, she really didn't know. She didn't even know the name of the village the campsite was in. It wasn't like she was lost or anything. She could easily ask the barman the name of the place and probably get him to call her a taxi back to the campsite if it came to that. It was just a strange situation to be in. It certainly wasn't how she imagined spending the second night of her engagement.

After a moment longer, she picked up her glass and took a long sip. When she was done, she moved to put the glass down only to change her mind and take another sip, this one even longer than the first.

'I'm sure they're not worth it.'

Daisy looked up to find the barman staring straight at her.

You could tell the restaurant was swanky from his clothes – a sharp white shirt with brightly coloured braces of all things.

'Who said I was drinking because of man problems?'

'Well, I didn't. I was thinking it might have been a terrible boss or something, but now, judging by the way you responded, I would say it's definitely a man. But my statement still stands. He's not worth it.'

Daisy lifted the drink back to her lips, only this time she didn't take a sip. Instead, she let out a deep breath that steamed up the inside of the cold glass. The thing was, she wasn't sure whether the barman was right or not. If you had asked her forty-eight hours ago, she would have said he was certainly wrong. Theo, she had believed, was the best guy she had ever met, but was that just an illusion she had wanted to see? Was the fact she had said yes to spending the rest of her life with him all it took to reveal the real him? The him that would put words in her mouth? Perhaps the ring hadn't been a forgotten error, and he remembered his proposal to Heather all along. And if that was the case, did she really know the man she planned on marrying at all?

'You know, I'm a good listener,' the barman said. 'Comes with the job. You wouldn't be the first person to sit on one of those stools and unload.'

Daisy scoffed. There was no way she wanted to share the intimacies of her relationship with this complete stranger, she thought, only for her to consider the idea for a moment longer. The problem with talking with any of her friends or her mum was that they already knew Theo. They, like her, might be able to dismiss things as a one-off or be clouded by their own preconceptions of the man they knew. Perhaps a stranger's opinion was exactly what she needed.

'Okay,' she said, putting her glass down and straightening her back as she looked at the barman. 'Maybe you can answer a question for me?'

'I can definitely try.'

She nodded before taking another quick sip of her drink, although this time, it was more for courage than any other reason.

'Would you propose to a girl with the same ring you had already used to propose to another who had said no, years beforehand?'

The barman's eyes widened as silence punctuated the end of her question.

'Jeez,' he said finally. 'It's a good thing you ordered the bottle.'

40

Daisy blew out a long breath, which quickly turned into a sigh. And all the while, the barman was staring at her, shaking his head ever so slightly as if in disbelief.

'So, man problems then,' he chuckled. It was a sweet laugh, clearly designed to break the tension. 'I'm not sure how to respond to that one, other than no. Definitely not.'

Daisy lowered her eyes back to the bar as her stomach sank. It was the answer she had known she was going to get. Probably the answer she had wanted to get too, but that didn't mean it felt any better. For a minute, all she could do was stare at her glass and try to ignore the gnawing in her gut.

After another sip of her drink, she looked up, ready to explain the situation a little further, only to find the barman was gone. A quick glance was all it took to locate him further down the bar, pouring a pint. He flashed her a smile, conveying he hadn't forgotten her, then carried on serving the other customer.

It was probably wrong, Daisy thought, not to give any context when talking about the ring, most notably that it had come from Theo's grandmother, but as it happened, she hadn't needed to.

When the barman returned, he was the one with questions for her.

'Does this ring have sentimental value?' he said. 'I mean, I was thinking about it just then, and if it's some ring he just picked out from a high-street jeweller, then that is a definite red flag. But maybe if it's like a family heirloom—'

'It was his grandmother's,' Daisy cut in.

The barman let out a long vowel sound. 'Ahhh,' he said. 'Then that makes things a bit different. I'm not sure how I would respond to that.'

Given that Daisy was no wiser than she had been before, she switched up her questions to ask him something different.

'Okay, would you tell a girl you were dating that you had proposed to someone before? Or would you just hope they didn't find out?'

'Ouch.' The barman gave a visible flinch. 'This is getting worse and worse. I feel like I should give you a drink on the house, but I'll be honest, I probably shouldn't let you drink more than one bottle.'

Daisy let out a sad half chuckle.

'But would you?' she said. 'You're meant to be open in relationships, aren't you? Tell them everything?'

The barman shrugged a little as he pondered this question.

'I'm not sure it's quite so simple,' he said. 'I mean, I've only been with my girlfriend a few months, but I have a lot of respect for her. That doesn't mean I'm going to go home tonight and tell her I spent the evening listening to a beautiful woman in a mess over a guy who probably doesn't deserve her.'

Daisy wasn't sure which part of the comment shocked her more: the fact the barman had called her beautiful – which she sure as hell didn't feel after the day she'd had – or that he'd said Theo didn't deserve her. Then again, it was probably easy to make a judgement based on the information she had just told him. Wasn't that why she had asked his opinion, after all?

'So why wouldn't you tell her?' Daisy asked.

'Because it doesn't matter. You don't matter.'

'Thanks,' Daisy said, not sure she'd ever gone from being completely flattered to completely offended so quickly before.

The man read her expression.

'I don't mean to sound like a dick,' he said. 'And if I knew you better, it would be completely different. But as it stands, it's true. I talk to people on a daily basis. Make them feel listened to. Heard. You're not the first person who has sat at this bar and poured their heart out, and a few of those have made some very inappropriate offers at the end of the night. Offers I suspect some men may have taken them up on. Sometimes, I tell my girlfriend about them, but mostly not. There's no point. It doesn't matter what these women say; I'm never going to go home with them. Either the trust is there or it isn't. That's what it comes down to, for me at least. Obviously, every relationship is different.'

Daisy sat back against the barstool, the question weighing heavily on her mind. Did she trust Theo? She came back to the same answer: twenty-four hours ago, twelve hours ago even, the answer had been yes. But it only took a moment, a split second, for an illusion to be shattered. She opened her mouth, ready to ask the barman yet another question, when a different voice spoke.

'I don't suppose you'd mind if I grab a glass to help you out with that wine, would you?'

41

Theo looked terrible. His skin was ashen and his shoulders sagged, as if they were being pushed down by some invisible weight.

'Daisy, I am so sorry,' he said. 'Please, can I just have five minutes to explain? I was horrible, and I was wrong, and I know I was well out of line with some of the things I said. Please, could you just hear me out?'

Daisy looked at the wine bottle. It was still over half full, and having paid for it, she had no intention of leaving any. Yet, rather than replying to Theo, her eyes drifted up towards the barman. Given how Daisy had just spent the last half an hour detailing everything that had happened, she didn't doubt that he had put two and two together and figured out who Theo was. And while she knew nothing about the man other than his job, she somehow sensed he would know the right thing to do.

'There's a table that's just come free in the restaurant,' he said, gesturing with a nod of his head. 'It's got a good view, if you want somewhere nice to sit?'

'Thank you,' Theo said.

Daisy wasn't sure it was the response she expected the barman to give, but she had already made up her mind to go with whatever he said, mainly because it took the weight of deciding out of her hands.

'Fine,' she said to Theo, picking up her bottle of wine. 'But if I don't like what you have to say, you can get me another bottle and I will drink it by myself.'

With that, she marched off, not entirely sure where she was going until she reached the restaurant and spotted the lone free table in the corner by the window. For a split second, she thought a member of staff was going to tell her that the table was reserved, but no one did and so she took a seat.

A moment after she had sat down, Theo appeared with an empty wine glass in his hand. Without a word, he took the seat opposite her, then silently filled up his glass, before he gently placed the bottle down on the table between them and let out a deep sigh.

'I was a dick,' he said.

Daisy scoffed.

'That's more polite than I would've put it,' she replied.

Deep sadness shrouded his expression. 'I'm sorry. I think it was just everything with my parents. All the tension from the day just built up and I let it out in the worst possible way.'

'And at the wrong person?' Daisy pointed out.

'I know. I know about that. But believe me, I just don't know how to react to them when they behave like that. When my mother just can't see reason. It's like she gets tunnel vision and I just let it get to me.'

Not for the first time, Daisy wondered about all the time Theo had spent in the house when he was collecting the camping gear. She could only imagine the things his mother had said to him during that time.

'What else did they say?' Daisy asked.

'You don't want to know,' he replied.

Daisy thought about the comment. As strange as it was, she actually did want to know, because knowing for certain had to be better than imagining all the ways his family could have insulted her.

'You don't have to tell me if you don't want to, but I'll just make my own assumptions if you don't,' she said, voicing her thoughts.

'Daisy, I don't want to do this.'

'Can I make a wild guess and assume that children came into the conversation? Judging from the way you reacted to us talking about them.'

For the first time, Theo reached down, took hold of his glass and took an exceptionally long sip.

'Everything came into the conversation,' he said when he finished. 'I'm sorry, Daisy. I really thought it would be a positive experience. And then, seeing Heather, I didn't mean that to hurt you. It's just that she and I cut things off so abruptly, and I felt so terrible for how it ended between us. Then, when you said she was happy, and married and pregnant, it was like this massive weight had been lifted from my shoulders. Like I didn't need to feel guilty any more. But I needed to see her, to be sure, you know, to make sure she really was okay. I guess I didn't think about how that would be for you, after everything you'd already gone through with my family.'

Daisy should have known Theo never thought of himself first. Of course he had been thinking about Heather, and making things right there, just like he had been thinking about keeping his family included in his life by wanting to share the proposal with them, regardless of how they acted.

Still, Daisy remained silent for a while longer before she spoke.

'But if this massive weight had lifted, why did we end up in a fight about it?'

Theo nodded as if validating her question, though it still took a couple of moments longer before he spoke.

'You're right. Heather was good. She was *so* good. And I was happy for her, I *am* happy for her, but we had a couple of drinks and reminisced a bit. You know, talked about how life used to be and I couldn't help but hear my mother's voice in my ear.'

'Saying that I wasn't good enough?' Daisy finished for him.

Theo frowned. 'It wasn't that. Not entirely. It was that she didn't understand how we felt we could know each other well enough to get married. Dad and her met at university, you see. They had five years together before he proposed. And even though the proposal to Heather didn't mean anything like it did with you, we had known each other for two decades when I asked.'

'So that's what scared you. That we don't know each other well enough to get married?'

At her words, Theo reached across and took hold of Daisy's hands. 'No, I don't think that for a second. I have messed things up. I know that. But Daisy, that proposal is the most certain I have been of anything in my life. When I said I wanted to spend the rest of my life with you, that wasn't just some flippant remark. I've imagined it, so many times. You and I growing old together. Throwing the crusts of our morning toast off the boat to ducks and swans, while the grandchildren sit on our laps – if we decided to have them, of course. I don't mind either way. I've seen it. You and I together, taking the boats on the canals up and down the country and travelling other places too. Taking flights to Asia, or Australia perhaps. I thought about how, when I get tired of running up and down the canals day in day out, we could convert another boat, and have it as a sit-in café that I can serve in. Or we could both sell up and do something else entirely. I've imagined you, grey-haired, glasses on the end of your nose as I bring you cups of tea and try not to disturb your painting, and taking ballroom dancing lessons together in some old, cold village hall.'

'Ballroom dancing?' Daisy said, raising her eyebrows.

Theo shook his head and let out a light chuckle, although it was laced with sadness.

'What I'm trying to say is whenever I imagine my future, Daisy May, the one thing that is constant, is you. The children, the place, the careers don't matter. You and me, that's what matters. Whenever, wherever. It's always you and I. That's all that counts. So I am so sorry. Honestly, I will do anything you ask for me to prove how sorry I am. Please, please Daisy can you forgive me for being such an idiot?'

Theo took a breath in and in the silence, he stared at Daisy, waiting. Her throat suddenly felt inexplicably dry and by impulse, she reached for her glass, and yet she found it empty. Stretching out her arm, she went to pick up the bottle from the cooler, only to change her mind.

'Well, when you speak like that, how can I not?'

42

They left the restaurant together, Theo's arm looped around Daisy's waist, her weight propped up on him. They had opted for another bottle after they finished the first, during which time Theo filled Daisy in on some of the things his mother had said. Things that made Daisy's jaw tighten and fists clench, although she was grateful he told her.

Lines like, *Why did we spend so much on a private education for you to marry a waitress?* and, *Surely you must struggle to have an intelligent conversation with someone who doesn't even have a university degree.*

It was about his mother and not Daisy, Theo said time and again, and Daisy could see that. It wouldn't have mattered who Theo had brought through the door that morning; Daisy was certain Penelope would have found something wrong with them. She had never wanted to welcome Daisy into her home, but at the end of the day, it didn't matter. All that mattered was what Daisy and Theo thought of one another. And what the mess of the last day was teaching her was that she loved him. She loved him with her whole heart. She loved him because of the mistakes he made, because of how he only ever really got things wrong because he was trying too hard to get everything right. Without doubt, Daisy knew that she loved Theo more than she had known it was possible to love someone. And she was pretty sure that Theo felt the same.

'You two have a good night,' the barman said, throwing Daisy a smile as they left.

'Thank you,' she said, holding his gaze long enough for him to understand the gratitude wasn't solely about his farewell.

Despite the summer heat, there was a crisp chill blowing off the lake as they walked back to the campsite. Although Daisy barely felt it, what with the wine warming her from the inside and Theo's arm keeping the rest of her protected from the breeze.

'I was thinking,' Theo said as they stood for a moment and watched the moonlight reflect off the gentle ripples. 'There are some lovely jewellers in town. Maybe tomorrow we could go and take a look. You could pick out a ring that you like. That's yours and *only* yours.'

Daisy glanced down at her hand. She had yet to take the ring off her finger, but that was mostly because she had been worried that it would fall off in the grass and she wouldn't be able to find it. Whether or not she wanted it to be the ring that she wore forever as a sign of her love for Theo, she wasn't sure. Maybe something they picked out together, to remind her of how strong they could be when days got rough, would be a much better fit.

'That would be nice,' she said, then reached up onto her tiptoes and kissed him. 'But now, we should get into that tent of ours. It seemed pretty small, though. I'm not sure how we're both going to fit inside it.'

'Trust me.' Theo grinned at her. 'We'll find a way.'

43

For most people, waking up camping was probably the height of peace. Filling your lungs with crisp, clean air while listening to the bird calls and the lapping water on the lake were likely idyllic. But for Daisy, it was what she woke up to everyday. Of course, there were some subtle differences, like the damp, solid earth she was sitting on, the hills in front of her, shrouded in a thin veil of mist, and the children having an early-morning football game right outside their tent. Yes, that was a noise she wasn't used to waking up to.

'I bought some pastries,' Theo said, when he returned from having a quick shower, 'but maybe we'd be better off driving to Kendall and getting brunch there? We can save the pastries for the drive back tomorrow. I'm sure they'll keep just fine.'

'Breakfast in a café sounds great,' Daisy said as she stretched out the cricks in her neck.

She and Theo had talked for hours when they returned to the tent. He had told her why he was so keen to have children – he and his sister had been incredibly close growing up, even if they weren't now. As a child, it meant he'd always had a friend to do things with and his sister knew, even now, that if she needed him, he would be there. Daisy explained why she wasn't sure – she enjoyed her freedom, her business, and she wasn't entirely certain she was patient enough to be a mother. But she also reasoned that she felt too young to make that decision at the moment.

But then there was the other issue. One she'd never mentioned to Theo, though it hung around at the back of her mind, lingering in the shadows every time she thought about having children.

'Mum struggled after I was born,' Daisy said, recalling what her mother had told her about the year after Daisy's birth. 'She struggled so much that she left me. She moved to a different country without me, because she couldn't cope. And even though I don't remember it – I mean, I didn't even know it had happened until a couple of years ago – I still worry. I'm scared that will happen to me too.'

It was odd how hard she found admitting the truth to herself as much as to Theo. And it wasn't like the worry went away, just because she had said the words aloud.

'It might,' Theo said honestly. 'But it might not. And even if it does, it wouldn't be the same. There's more support out there for mothers who are struggling now. Not to mention that it's something we would both be watching out for. We would make sure we're prepared so that it never got to the way it was with your mum. But that's only if you decide you want to have children, of course. I'm not trying to pressure you at all. I'm just trying to make you see that your mum's past doesn't have to affect your decision.'

It was a grown-up discussion. A weighing of pros, cons, and emotions for the both of them. It was the type of conversation they should probably have had before Theo had proposed, but the fact they had come back from the brink, to have that type of conversation at all, proved, in Daisy's mind, why they could absolutely make the marriage work.

It took less than half an hour to pack everything up into the car, and for a moment, Daisy wondered if Theo was going to mention saying goodbye to Heather. She would have been okay if he wanted to, she decided, but was a little grateful that he didn't even mention his ex's name.

'Have you thought about what you want?' Theo said instead, as they drove towards Kendall.

'For breakfast, you mean?' Daisy asked.

'No, I mean for an engagement ring. Have you thought about what type of ring you want? There are a couple of new jewellers and some antique and artisan ones, if you fancy something different.'

Daisy hadn't really considered what type of ring she would pick for herself, although given that it would be the one accessory she wore for her entire life, it was probably important not to rush into it.

'I don't know. I guess I'll know when I see it,' she said.

Two hours later, after a breakfast of eggs Benedict with an extra hash brown, Daisy discovered it wasn't quite that simple.

'Is it me, or do loads of these just look the same?' she said. They were inside a prestigious jeweller's that boasted over a thousand engagement rings, though the problem – in Daisy's mind, at least – was that there wasn't much difference from one to the next.

At least 30 per cent of them were solitaires. Sure, there was some variation in terms of size and shape of the stone, or thickness of the band, and there was yellow gold, white gold, or platinum to choose from. Although the platinum and the white gold looked identical, so it didn't feel like there was much variation there either.

'These are classic styles,' the jeweller said, with a slight hint of snootiness, clearly not approving of Daisy's remark. 'Though if you're after something a little more flamboyant, we have several halo rings in stock.'

Daisy wasn't sure if flamboyant was what she was after at all, but she smiled at the jeweller, who took it as a sign to fetch yet another tray of rings.

Halo, Daisy discovered, meant even more diamonds. A ring of small stones, set around a central larger one. Of course, some of the diamonds were square-shaped, some were oval, and there were still the same variations in band and stone size, but it was hardly a great selection, the way she had imagined a jeweller with one thousand engagement rings would have.

'That one's pretty,' Daisy said, picking one that seemed to be middling in everything. Medium-sized band. Medium-sized diamond. Medium size ring of diamonds around the middle.

'Ahh, yes, that one is lovely and very popular. Why don't you try it on? Of course, this one is just a guide. We will get it sized to fit you at no extra cost.'

Daisy looked at Theo, who nodded at her. A moment later, the jeweller was slipping the ring on her finger.

'It's very sparkly,' Daisy said, describing the ring with the first words that came to mind. And it was fitting. Every diamond on the ring glinted with its own spectrum, and the overall effect was mesmerising. 'It's beautiful,' she said, needing a more fitting adjective than 'sparkly'. It really was something. Feeling like perhaps this was the engagement ring she could spend the rest of her life wearing, she looked up at the jeweller.

'How much is it?' she asked.

44

Daisy was marching out of the shop. She wasn't entirely sure where she was going, she just knew that she needed to get away from the snooty jeweller with his extortionately priced rings.

'It's not that ridiculous, really,' Theo said. 'I mean, you're going to wear it every day for the rest of your life. It's not surprising that it would cost that much.'

'I could put a deposit down on a house for how much that ring cost,' Daisy said. 'And it wasn't like there weren't ones that were even bigger. There is no way I could wear something like that every day. I'd be terrified of losing it. No, I want something I can wear every day that doesn't cost an average salary.'

'That's obviously the going price for engagement rings nowadays,' Theo replied. He didn't seem half as upset about the situation as Daisy was. In fact, he was giving the impression that it really wasn't that big a deal.

'Maybe the average price for people who have more money than sense,' Daisy replied. 'No, absolutely not.'

They walked a few steps further, and it was only when Theo

slipped his hand in hers and tugged it ever so slightly, that Daisy realised how fast she had been walking.

'Okay,' Theo said, pulling her around slightly so that he was looking at her. 'Then maybe we should check out the antique shops instead. There are loads of beautiful antique rings. After all, the one you're wearing is antique, and you liked that one, didn't you?'

Daisy glanced down at the ring on her finger. It was true – if she ignored the negative associations with it, it really was stunning. So maybe an antique ring was the answer.

'Okay, let's try that,' she said, and let Theo lead her into a small, cabinet-filled antique shop.

Unlike at the previous jewellers, the prices were all displayed and, just like Theo had suggested, there were lots more in the budget range that Daisy was after. But as she tried on what had to be her tenth ring, Daisy found herself faced with another problem.

'I feel like they've all got their own story. Is that weird?' she said, as she slipped an emerald and white-gold ring onto her finger. 'Like they all had a life before me that I'm somehow interrupting.'

'Yes, it is. Very weird,' Theo said.

She punched Theo lightly on the shoulder before sliding the ring off her finger and handing it back to the jeweller.

'They've all already got their own history,' Daisy said with a sigh as she looked at Theo. 'It's different with the ring from your grandmother. You knew her story. You knew how many happy memories she had because of the ring.'

Theo frowned. 'Actually, she got divorced. She mainly kept the ring in her jewellery box until she gave it to my mum.'

'What, and you didn't think that was important?' Daisy said, shocked that Theo would not see that as an issue. Though, from what she had learned about Theo over the last weekend, she knew she shouldn't be surprised. 'That's the problem with all the jewellery in here,' she said, waving her hand dramatically to take in as much of the shop as she could. 'You don't know how many rings here are from people who weren't happily married. Or had to pawn their jewellery because they ran out of money, or belonged to people who have died.'

'Well, considering the majority of pieces here are well over a hundred years old, I'm guessing most of the owners are dead. Or in the *Guinness Book of Records*,' Theo replied.

Daisy chose not to respond to that.

'I want a ring that's our story. Just yours and mine.'

'Well then, let's go back to the other jeweller's,' Theo said. 'I really don't care what it costs. This is the only ring I'm ever going to buy, after all.'

Still, Daisy shook her head. 'No. There's no way I'm paying those prices. We are not starting our married life in debt because of a single piece of jewellery,' Daisy replied. 'No, we just have to wait.'

'Until what?'

'Until the right thing turns up.'

'The right thing that isn't new or antique? Not exactly sure how that's going to happen, Daisy.'

She sucked on the inside of her cheek, but there was no way she was going to change her mind on it.

'Look,' Theo said, 'I don't mean to push, but you are my fiancé, right?'

'Yes,' Daisy said, although it still sounded strange, hearing him say the word.

'Right, and I would like my fiancé to have a ring. If you don't want to wear the one from my grandmother, pick something. Pick something cheap, because I think it's going to take years to get what you're after. And I'm willing to wait, I am. But I still want people to see you with a ring on your finger.'

'What, so they know I'm yours?' Daisy said, leaning in up against him.

'Too right.' He bent down towards her, and the smile that played on his lips was irresistible. Daisy pushed up on her tiptoes, ready to lose herself in his kiss, when a throat cleared behind her.

Blushing, the pair turned to look at the jeweller, whose face was pinched and expression stony.

'If it is budget rings you are after, we have a selection of costume jewellery on the other side of the shop.'

45

Twenty minutes later, Daisy left the antique jewellery shop with a new, temporary engagement ring. It was gold-plated with a cubic zirconia stone cut in a square shape. To Daisy's untrained eye, it looked remarkably similar to many of the ones in the expensive first shop.

'We will get you something real as soon as you find it,' Theo said. 'And budget really isn't an issue.'

'I like this one,' Daisy said, stretching out her fingers so that the stone caught the sunlight and glittered even more than it did in the shop. She had decided on the second costume piece she tried on, mainly because it was a decent fit, but the more she looked at it, the more she liked it. Of course, getting a real diamond that size was out of the question.

'I get that you like it,' Theo said. 'But I'm pretty sure it's going to turn your finger green at some point. And I don't think the stone is meant to wobble like that either. Still, it's nice seeing you smiling after yesterday.'

'Am I smiling?' Daisy said. Only then did she become aware of the ache that was spreading across her cheeks. The type of ache that only settled after an extended time spent grinning like a Cheshire cat. With a newfound lightness in her chest, she tightened her grip around Theo's arm. Together, they wandered up and down the little streets, their paces perfectly matched as they walked. Occasionally, they stopped to look in shop windows or browse inside one or two, but there was no urgency to the way they were moving. Their only purpose was being together, until a little before midday when Theo suddenly stopped and looked at his watch.

'Wow, we should get going,' Theo said. 'The hotel's a forty-five-minute drive from here, and they said we could check in early, you know, because they didn't have a room last night.'

'That's nice of them,' Daisy said, already knowing that the evening was going to go far smoother than it had yesterday.

'Right?' Theo agreed. 'I also mentioned that we got engaged on Friday, so fingers crossed, they are going to throw in a bottle of wine for us, too.'

A bottle of wine, Theo, and no one to disturb them. It almost sounded too good to be true.

46

Given how she knew Theo wanted the weekend to be memorable, and not just because of his family, Daisy suspected the hotel he'd booked would be something special. But the reality blew her out of the water.

The check-in had involved a drive through the extensive country grounds before a short walk into reception, where they were met with cold towels and a glass of freshly squeezed orange juice. Then it was a trip up a winding staircase, where a crystal chandelier hung from the ceiling and the walls were lined with modern, abstract oil paintings. Daisy had wanted to spend a little longer just looking at them, making note of the technique and the skill and the way the images changed when she looked at them from a different angle. But the porter was standing by the door to their room and she didn't want to keep him waiting.

'After you,' he said, pushing open the door, then stepping aside so that Daisy could enter.

'Wow,' she said, feeling her jaw drop.

'If you need anything, just ring down to reception,' the man said.

'Thank you, we will,' Theo replied.

'And your spa session is booked for 2 p.m.'

It took Daisy a moment for the words to register.

'Spa session?' She turned around to look at the man, but he was already out of the door and closing it behind him. 'Theo,' she said, after a pause, 'this is way too much.'

The four-poster bed had been adorned with a heart made of rose petals and a small brown bear, with a little paper tag saying that he was theirs to keep, sat in the centre. There was also a platter of chocolate-covered strawberries and an array of candles that had already been lit, sending tendrils of lavender-scented smoke into the air. Rather than the bottle of wine Theo had hoped for, it was a bottle of Champagne which sat in the wine cooler.

'You really didn't have to do all this,' Daisy said as she leant in and kissed Theo, only for him to break away sooner than she had expected.

'Yeah, about that,' Theo said. 'I don't think I did.' Rather than reciprocating Daisy's excitement, he looked mildly concerned.

'What do you mean?'

'I mean, I booked the hotel and everything, and told them I had just proposed, but this is pricey Champagne, and I know I didn't book us into the spa. I was going to wait to see if you wanted to go first.'

'You think the hotel did this?' Daisy said, feeling her forehead crumple with confusion.

'It seems a bit extravagant for a hotel to put on, even for a proposal,' Theo replied.

Daisy looked again at the spread before them. The strawberries were perfectly ripe and she could smell the freshness rising from them, but it was only when she went to pick one off the platter that she saw the envelope propped up against the wine cooler.

'It's addressed to both of us, first names only,' she said, picking it up and showing it to Theo.

She ran her finger beneath the seal and opened the envelope before pulling out the note. As she read it, warmth filled her chest and a light chuckle escaped her lips.

'Here, have a read,' she said, handing it to Theo. A moment later, he let out a light laugh that was remarkably similar to hers.

Wanted you guys to have the best weekend possible.

  Enjoy yourselves.

  Bex and Claire

  P.S. We paid for all this from the money we took from the coffee shop this weekend. Sorry about that.

'Enjoy ourselves?' Theo said, placing the letter back down by the strawberries while raising an eyebrow. 'Any ideas on how we can entertain ourselves in this gigantic room with its mammoth four-poster bed?'

'Oh, I don't know,' Daisy said, a smirk twisting up on her lips. 'You're going to have to let me think about that for a moment.'

47

Daisy didn't want to leave the room, but the spa was beckoning and, just like the rest of the hotel, the experience was sublime. Built in the basement, with red brick walls and a variety of hot tubs and saunas, every little room and pool seemed to have a different scent, with each one more divine than the last.

'Wow, I didn't know how much I needed a massage,' Daisy said as the pair sat in a pool together after their treatments. 'I don't think I've ever felt that relaxed in my life.' Every muscle in her body had been scrubbed, moisturised and pummelled. And after a night out camping on the hard ground, it had been just the thing to work out the knots in her back.

'I know what you mean. I could happily go straight back to bed and not get up till morning,' Theo replied.

'That sounds like a good idea to me.' Daisy grinned. 'We've still got half a bottle of Champagne left. And a couple of strawberries, too.'

'We can't spend the entire time in the room, you know,' Theo said, arching one of his eyebrows as he spoke.

'Why not?'

'Well, to start with, I picked this place because of the grounds. We have to at least go for a walk, and we've got a reservation for dinner at eight too.'

'Fine,' Daisy said, leaning forward in the water, as if she was going to kiss Theo, only to splash water at him instead.

'Hey! You know I'm not going to let you get away with that, right?'

A moment later, he was chasing Daisy around the pool. The pair laughed and shrieked as they continued to splash about, ducking and diving beneath the water, until eventually Theo caught up with her, scooped her into his arms and kissed her passionately on the lips.

'You know, I don't think today could get any better,' Daisy said when they finally broke apart.

'I know what you mean,' Theo replied. 'Although you're only saying that because you haven't seen the maze yet.'

'There's a maze?'

'There is. There's a maze, peacocks, a lake with swans and geese and even a little church. I thought there were lots of opportunities for photos here, so when we get back to Wildflower Lock, you could do some paintings of the place.'

Daisy looked back at Theo, even more stunned than she had been at the discovery of the maze. 'You chose this place so there would be lots of things for me to paint?'

'Is that all right?'

'It's better than all right,' she said. 'It's absolutely perfect.'

With her heart the fullest it had ever been, she pushed up on her toes as if she was about to kiss Theo, only when their lips were less than an inch apart, she flung her hands through the water and splashed him once again.

'Last one out of the maze is the loser!' she yelled, bolting for the steps out of the pool.

48

As it happened, they left the maze at exactly the same time. By the time they had showered and dressed, they left the hotel building together, although Daisy didn't let up, racing Theo all the way to the twists and turns of hedgerow which were situated towards a large lake, not even stopping to look at the peacocks. After all, she figured they would still be there when she came back out. But despite a slight head start, a couple of wrong turns meant she and Theo were quickly reunited, at which point they continued to make their way through together.

'I don't know if I've ever been in a maze before,' Theo said as they reached the centre.

Unlike the outside, which had been solely green, the prize for reaching the centre was an explosion of colour. A large fountain, covered in blue and white mosaics, glinted in the afternoon sun, while butterflies flittered between the bright-purple buddleia bushes and vibrant red and yellow roses.

'You must have been in a maze before,' Daisy said in disbelief as she took a seat on one of the benches. 'Surely you visited one when you were a child?'

'I guess so. Probably. But I don't remember it. I like that, though. I like that the first time I'll ever remember going through a maze was with you. This weekend. It makes it feel even more special.'

As he gazed at Daisy, she could feel the love in his eyes so fiercely that it burned in her heart. It seemed ridiculous that less than a day ago, she had been questioning whether they should be together.

'It feels a bit like a metaphor for our relationship, don't you think?' Daisy said.

'Why's that?'

'You know, it may have taken us one or two wrong turns but we know that if we keep going through it together, we'll always find our way out.'

The more she spoke, the more she realised how true the words felt to her, yet as she finished, she found Theo staring at her with a pinched brow.

'What, what is it? Did I say something ridiculous? I did, didn't I?' Daisy could feel a flush of embarrassment colour her cheeks. 'Ignore what I said.'

Theo shook his head. 'No, you're completely right,' he said. 'It's not ridiculous at all. It's a maze. Life's a maze. The only thing is, I don't think it matters whether we make our way out of it. All that matters is that if we are stuck in it, we are stuck together.'

Daisy had lost count of the number of times she had felt her cheeks aching with a smile that day, and yet once again, there was nothing she could do to stop it.

'You are so soppy, you know that right?'

'Only with you.'

For a minute, it felt like nothing in the world mattered. Just the two of them, there, kissing in the middle of a maze.

Daisy would have happily forgone dinner entirely and stayed there until sunset, but it was Theo who broke away.

'Come on,' he said. 'We need to get out of here. There's a church on the grounds. I thought we could check it out. You know, potential wedding venues and everything.' He flashed her a quick grin before bolting back into the maze, ready to find his way out, with Daisy hot on his heels.

49

The rest of the time at the hotel went by like an absolute dream. After the walk, during which Daisy must have taken a hundred photos of birds and plants, she indulged in such a long soak in the roll-top bath that they were late for their dinner reservation. Thankfully, the staff were wonderful, as was the four-course menu.

'I feel like I've got a lot to learn in the kitchen still,' Daisy said as she took the last mouthful of the most divine lemon tart she had ever tried.

'Well, if you need someone to taste-test, you know I'm always here for you.'

'What a gentleman,' Daisy laughed.

The bed, as Daisy could've predicted merely from looking at it, was the most comfortable she had ever slept on, and when sunlight filtered through the curtains, stirring her from sleep, she had no desire to leave. No desire to uncurl herself from Theo's arms and get up. Thankfully, having foreseen Daisy's reluctance to get out of the bed, Theo had arranged for them to have room-service breakfast. A tray full of freshly baked pastries, fruit and yogurts, along with strong coffee and fresh juices, was exactly the thing her body desired. It was the antithesis of the night before, both the tent and the argument, and even when they drove back towards Wildflower Lock, with Daisy's fingers interlocked over Theo's on the gearstick, it felt as if the world was almost perfect. Almost.

They were still two hours away from home when Theo's phone buzzed on the dashboard yet again. Daisy had lost count of how many times his phone had rung, but it had to be reaching double figures. And it was the same people trying to get through every time.

'You really need to speak to them,' Daisy said. 'I get you don't want me to listen in on speakerphone while we're driving, but why don't you pull over at the next service station? You can ring them back.'

'Anything my parents want to say, they can say in front of you too,' he said. 'But it doesn't matter what they've got to say, I don't want to hear it. They made their opinion on the matter clear, and they can deal with the consequences.'

His eyes remained fixed on the road for a split second longer before he turned back to Daisy and flashed her a smile.

'It's all right, honestly. The way I see it, we've got one of two outcomes: either my parents realise how nasty they have been, they apologise to you genuinely, and we work towards building bridges, or they don't. And if they don't, well, that's it. I don't want that kind of negativity brought into our lives and our family,' he said, a look of fear flashing on his face. 'I mean us. We are a family. Even if it's just the two of us. Well, three. Johnny too, of course.'

As much as Daisy agreed about Johnny being an integral part of the family, she wasn't going to be swayed by Theo's diversion tactics. 'I know what you meant, but frankly, you're essentially making me the reason you lose contact with your parents. They're not going to be too keen on that. And how do you know they're not ringing to apologise now?'

Theo slowed down slightly before he turned to look Daisy swiftly in the eye. 'I love that you are still trying to think the best of them, but how many times have my parents come down to Wildflower Lock since you've known me?'

'Well, never.'

'Or to Slimbridge when I lived there? It wasn't much closer, but it was closer. They still didn't come. Relationships are a two-way street; you showed that to me more than ever.'

'Me?'

'Of course you. You came to London to make things work for us. You sacrificed being together so I could carry on with my job and waited for me until a chance came for me to move back. You put the effort in to make this relationship work.'

'That's just what a good girlfriend does,' Daisy said. 'It's what a good person does when they love someone.'

'Exactly.'

The mood in the car shifted ever so slightly, and the last thing Daisy wanted was for Theo's parents to pull down the atmosphere when they had been having such an incredible time, and so she turned the conversation to the most obvious topic she could think of.

'I guess as we still have a couple of hours' driving ahead of us, we should do some planning.'

'Planning?' he said.

'The wedding. I mean, you do actually want to get married, right? You're not one of these people who wants us to be fiancés for the rest of our lives, are you?'

Daisy knew people like that, of course – people who remained engaged indefinitely, with no intention of taking the next step, but she had never imagined herself or Theo as one of those. Still, it was a relief when he spoke next.

'No, I definitely want to get married.'

'Great,' Daisy chuckled. 'So that's the first thing we're agreed on.'

'And I'm not one of these people who wants to have a ridiculously long engagement either,' Theo said.

'Me too,' Daisy replied, 'so we agree on that too.' She was about to continue with her next question when she paused, discovering she still needed further clarification on the previous point. 'Just to check, how long do you think is "ridiculously long"?'

Theo shrugged a little, throwing her a quick glance as he continued to drive.

'I don't know. I think waiting for two years seems a long time. I guess I was thinking maybe next summer would work for the wedding.'

Daisy wrinkled her nose.

'Summer is the busiest time of the year for me. And we're probably going to want to take some time off afterwards to travel. I don't know if I can risk closing down the business then. Certainly not for very long.'

'Good point.' Theo nodded in agreement. 'So next spring or autumn?'

'I'd be inclined to go for autumn,' Daisy replied. 'It's normally quite good weather then. And I like autumn flowers.'

'Perfect,' he said. 'Then I guess the first thing we need to start thinking about venues.'

'And there's no time like the present,' Daisy grinned as she took out her phone and began to type away.

50

Since starting the business, Daisy had been careful with money in ways she had never been before. She always knew how much was in each account and what date all her regular bills came out. She paid her credit card off in full each month and assuming there were no sudden unexpected expenses with the boat, she was confident she could put aside a couple of hundred pounds a month towards the wedding fund, but as she opened up her first venue and clicked on their prices, it didn't look like that type of money was going to go far.

'That can't be right. This place says it charges six grand to hire. And that's without food or music or even chairs and tables,' Daisy said.

'Well, they say weddings are expensive,' Theo replied. While it wasn't the most helpful comment, it did set Daisy's mind on a more practical line of thinking than just searching randomly for wedding venues and seeing what came up.

'How much do people normally spend on a wedding?' she said.

'I don't know, about ten grand?' he replied.

'Ten grand?'

Daisy's eyes widened. A couple of hundred quid a month definitely wasn't going to cut that. Did people really have ten grand lying around to spend on a wedding? Sure, she could understand how those in flamboyant marquees or country houses with five-course, sit-down dinners cost that, but she didn't need anything that elaborate. Just a nice venue to have some photos done and a place to dance away the night.

'I'm going to Google it. I want to see how much the average person spends,' she said, convinced that Theo's answer was way off the mark.

Yet Daisy had barely hit enter on the question when her stomach dropped out beneath her. 'Twenty-five grand,' she said. 'The average UK wedding costs twenty-five grand. That's ridiculous. I'd rather not get married than spend that amount of money.'

She had made the remark flippantly. In fact, she hadn't even really thought about it, but when she glanced over at Theo, she noticed the way his face had pinched.

'I guess it's just the little things that add up,' he said. 'Venues, save-the-date cards, bridesmaid dresses.'

'But I don't want any of that stuff,' Daisy said. 'I just want you and me at the wedding.'

'I don't think it's going to be quite that simple.'

'Why not?'

'Well, to start with, there are people we will have to invite. Go through your list.'

'My list?' Daisy said. 'You already know it: Bex, Claire, Ian and Amelia, and a plus-one for Bex if she's dating someone, then Mum and Nicholas.'

Those eyes widened. 'That can't be your entire guest list,' he said. 'There must be other people you want to invite. Yvonne, to start with.'

'Fine, yes, you're right. Maybe there are a couple of people on the lock, but that's it. Why, who were you planning on inviting? I guess we'll have to invite your parents and just wait and see if they come.'

At this, Theo's brow furrowed. 'Well, my cousins all invited me to their weddings, so I suspect they'll expect an invitation. Aunts and uncles, my godparents, my parents' close friends too. You know, I've always called quite a few people uncle and aunt, even if they're not blood relatives. I'm sure they'll be disappointed if they weren't invited.'

Daisy wondered if Heather's parents were included in that list, but she didn't say anything. Instead, what she said was, 'So you're saying that this wedding is going to be 90 per cent a get-together of all your family with 10 per cent people I want there.'

She didn't mean to sound churlish, particularly after the lovely day they'd had, but there was no way she was going to spend twenty grand on that. She could feel the tension brewing in the air, and knew she needed to break it before it settled. Thankfully, Theo got there first.

'Do you know what? You're right, it's completely fine. We'll do whatever we are both comfortable with. And we'll set a budget that you're happy with. Not that we need to worry that much; I've got a fair bit saved up.'

Daisy felt her head tilt to the side. 'How much is a "fair bit"?' she said, not sure why the comment had twisted her emotions so much.

'You know, just a bit.'

Daisy didn't know. Before *September Rose*, she hadn't had much in the way of real savings or equity, and even though she had the business, and a small excess if it was needed, she still worried.

'Theo, how much is "a bit"?' she repeated.

Theo's eyes remained forward until he glanced at Daisy with a slight bite down on his lip.

'A couple of hundred grand,' he said.

51

Daisy was sure she must have misheard. 'Sorry, did you say *grand* at the end there?' she said. 'As in two hundred thousand pounds? Pounds sterling?'

'Give or take,' Theo responded.

'I don't understand.'

That was all she could manage, but it was the truth. People didn't just have that amount of money in savings, did they? Okay, it wasn't like she'd worked her way up a career ladder or anything, but she had always been employed and no one could consider her work-shy and yet there was zero possibility of her having saved up that type of money. Even Bex, who had the most well-paid job of anyone she knew, had needed to scrimp and save to get a deposit for her flat in London. As far as Daisy was aware, Theo had never scrimped and saved, even though jobs on the canal didn't pay well at all. Certainly not enough for him to have saved up that sort of money.

'It's really come off investments,' he said. 'Well, some inheritance that I invested. When my grandfather left me some money, crypto was just taking off, so I put a few grand into that and it's done well.'

'A few grand?' Daisy questioned. To her, that meant two or three, not a quarter of a million pounds.

'It's not like I have an extravagant lifestyle or anything either, and I've always been that way. I've always saved rather than spent. I'm mean, you know when I bought the *Escape*, she was a shell, so I didn't need to dip into my savings then and I did all the work pretty cheaply.'

Of course, Daisy knew this about the *Narrow Escape*. Theo had kindly used all the skills he had learned doing up his own boat – and a couple of others too – to help with the *September Rose*, but that didn't change how at that precise moment she was having difficulty swallowing. Her throat had dried up entirely, and her mind was racing through what Theo's hidden wealth meant for her and their future.

Daisy could feel Theo's eyes flicking off the road to look at her, but she needed a moment to gather her thoughts before she spoke. It wasn't the immediate future that worried her so much as the distant one. She had no intention of leaving the canal any time soon. It was her business, her livelihood, and her life, but seeing Yvonne struggling had made Daisy realise there would be a time when dry land would be a more sensible idea and she would much rather make that move when she was young enough to enjoy that new chapter of her life. The problem was that when she had imagined her and Theo being in a place together, whether it was a boat or a house, it had been exactly that – together. Shared. Equal partners. How could they be equal if she wasn't able to contribute in the same way?

'I feel like I've said something to upset you,' Theo said. 'Should I have not told you? I didn't think it was a big deal. Unless you're sitting there thinking that you want to blow the entire lot on the wedding and honeymoon, that is. I might have a bit of a problem with that.'

'No. Trust me, that's not what I want to do,' Daisy said. 'I just hadn't really thought about how we were going to tackle finances when we got married.'

'We'll figure it out,' Theo said with an annoying nonchalance. Though Daisy wasn't convinced.

'Well, we really need to sort it out before we get married. I mean, where are we going to live? I really can't have Johnny in the *September Rose* with all the cooking I do, but is the *Escape* big enough for us to live in full-time?' Her head was spiralling with the logistics of it all. 'And I'm not sure I'd feel happy leaving the *September Rose* empty at nights either. Not every night. I mean, I know we do it a lot now, but I'm always there so early in the morning. Maybe we could see about getting a mooring next to each other—'

'Daisy.' Theo reached across and placed his hand on her lap. 'This is fine. It'll take us as long as it takes us, but we'll sort it out. And as for the money – if I thought it was going to be an issue, I wouldn't have mentioned it. I just wanted you to know that you don't have to miss out on anything, that's all. You don't have to feel like you need to cut back on the wedding because of money, that's all. I want you to have everything you want.'

Daisy pressed her lips tightly together. A wedding with everything she wanted. What did that mean? She wasn't sure, but for some reason, it still didn't make her feel good.

52

By the time they got back to Wildflower Lock, Daisy had discovered that weddings were probably the most ridiculously expensive events possible. She had found a website that listed all the things the day was supposed to include and had the average prices next to them, too. According to this site, the average bride spent over a thousand pounds on their wedding dress and five hundred on the cake. Well, Daisy decided, that was one way she would save money – getting her mother to bake it for her. Or if Pippa didn't want to, then she could even make it herself. And the rest of the food, too. But what about the venue and the music and all those other things? Those would be harder to find cheap options for, and could she really afford to do things on the cheap when the entirety of Theo's family were going to be there, judging her?

'Look, I think you're putting a bit too much pressure on yourself to get all this sorted as soon as possible,' Theo said. 'We've got all the time in the world. Isn't that the whole point of being engaged – to give yourself time to sort this?'

Daisy nodded.

'You're right,' she said, reaching across and squeezing his hand, though she still wasn't convinced it was true. The very first decision they had made about the wedding was that they didn't want to be engaged for years and that was even more true now than when they'd first discussed it. Thankfully, now they were back at the lock, there was a new thought which took priority.

'I can't wait to see Johnny,' she said, a lightness filling her chest at the thought of their canine companion. 'I hope he hasn't driven them mad.'

'I'm sure he's been spoiled rotten,' Theo replied. 'Especially if Amelia has been down.'

Daisy chuckled lightly because she knew it was true. As long as Claire and Ian refused to get a dog of their own, Amelia would make the most of every second she could with Daisy's. And Daisy understood. Even after the fancy hotel with the spa and luxury food, she wanted nothing more than a night curled up on the *Narrow Escape* with her feet on Theo and Johnny's head on her lap.

She took her bag from the boot of the car and was about to say as much to Theo, when a voice cut through the quiet.

'No, this is it. I mean it this time!'

The tone of the shout shot into the deepest recesses of Daisy's memory. Growing up, it felt like she had heard the same line spouted every other month in the same tone from the same person. She picked up her pace and raced through the gate from the car park to the canal.

'Mum?'

Her mother was marching out of the *Jeanette*, a heavy bag on her shoulders and her face contorted in anger.

'Mum, is everything okay?' Daisy asked.

Her mother turned to look at Daisy, sniffing back tears as she wiped her nose with the back of her hand.

'Daisy, thank goodness you're back,' she said, a look of relief washing over her. 'I'm going to need to stay at yours tonight.'

53

Everything seemed to happen so fast. One minute, Pippa was there, her arms wrapped tightly around Daisy, then the next moment she had spun on her heel and was marching up the towpath towards the *September Rose*. Still confused by what was going on, Daisy turned around to find Theo standing there. She wasn't exactly sure what she was going to say, but thankfully, he got there first.

'It's fine. You go be with your mum tonight. We've got plenty of time together.'

Daisy let out a groan. She had wanted to catch up with the girls. To thank them for taking care of the business, not to mention see Johnny after the weekend away, but she knew her mum and this situation too well.

'I'll come over to the *Escape* first,' she said. 'To give Mum some time to cool off before I try to talk to her. She's got her own key to the *September Rose*. I'm sure she'll let herself in.'

'Sounds like a good idea.'

A heavy weight filled Daisy's chest. So much for a night with her feet up on Theo and with Johnny's head on her lap. She watched until her mum had disappeared up ahead of her, then walked down to the lock and followed Theo over towards the *Narrow Escape*. They had barely set foot on the towpath when the barking started.

'I guess someone is pleased to see you,' Bex said as she appeared on the bow of the boat, only to be pushed to the side by Johnny as he leapt onto land before running back and forth between Daisy and Theo as if he couldn't decide which of them he wanted to greet first.

'It's good to see you too, boy,' Daisy said, crouching down and ruffling his fur. 'Yes, I've missed you too. We've both missed you lots. Have you been good? Have you been a good boy for everybody?'

While Daisy continued to fuss over Johnny, Theo walked over to greet their two-legged friends. It was only when Daisy finally looked up after several belly rubs and ear scratches that she saw they were all on the towpath and with their bags in their hands.

'You're not going already, are you?' Daisy said, leaving Johnny to run to Theo for attention. 'Do you not have time for a drink first? Just a quick one?'

It was unlike her friends to turn down the offer of a drink, be it a glass of wine or a cup of tea, but following her question, Bex and Claire exchanged a look that appeared close to a grimace, though it was Amelia who spoke first.

'I think they had enough drinks last night,' she said, in a voice that sounded more like the adult of the group than a child. 'Let's just say it's a good job I knew how to use your card machine, because if you'd left it up to them, you wouldn't have been paid for a single drink.'

Daisy looked at Claire, who raised her eyebrows and twisted her lips in response.

'That's not entirely true. We could have taken cash.'

'I don't think you were in any fit state to count properly,' Amelia said, shaking her head.

Daisy had no idea when Amelia had switched from being a young, carefree kid to this, but it was sweet how seriously she had taken her role in the coffee shop, even if she'd meant to be entertaining Johnny rather than working.

'Well, it sounds to me like you're the one who gets to keep all the tips,' Daisy replied.

'Oh, trust me, I have,' Amelia said. 'But we need to get off. I forgot to bring my homework. I need to get back so I can do it before tomorrow.'

At this, Claire stepped forward and wrapped her arms around Daisy in a tight hug. 'Next girls' weekend, she's staying with her father,' she said. Daisy let out a chuckle.

'We'll get together one evening in the week though, right?' Bex said, taking her turn to hug Daisy. 'Maybe you can come to my flat? Cocktails with a view? And then you can fill us in on... everything.'

'Oh, there's a lot to fill you in on, believe me,' Daisy said in a hushed voice. Although given the fuss that Theo was giving Johnny, she doubted he was listening to the conversation at all.

'Well, just give us a ring if you need to talk.'

'Will do,' Daisy replied. 'Why don't I walk back to the car with you?'

'Don't be silly, you've been travelling all day. You probably need to sit down.'

'Thank you. And thank you again for this weekend. And for everything with the proposal.'

'You're welcome.'

Claire was clearly about to go in for another hug, when from all the way up the towpath came Amelia's voice.

'Did you two not hear what I said about my homework? Come on! Hurry up!'

54

The boat was spotless. Claire and Bex both knew what a stickler Theo was for keeping things clean and tidy, and they had obviously tried their hardest to ensure that not a thing was out of place. The cushions were plumped up on the sofa, the coasters straight on the coffee table and even the floor had been mopped, although the minute Johnny raced inside, he left a trail of dust and leaves before flopping down on his bed.

'I feel you, Johnny,' Daisy said, taking off her shoes before dropping onto the sofa. 'That was definitely a weekend I won't forget.'

'I'm sorry,' Theo said, sitting down next to Daisy and shifting her around so that her legs lay across his lap. 'It wasn't exactly the weekend I'd planned.'

A pang of guilt struck in Daisy's chest. She hadn't meant to sound so negative.

'I meant the good things,' Daisy said, leaning across so that she could kiss him. 'I got to see where you grew up. And visit the Lake District and stay in the most beautiful hotel I've ever been in.'

'It was just the meeting my family, the used engagement ring, the ex-girlfriend, and the massive row that weren't so positive, right?'

Daisy let out a sad laugh. 'I think every couple has a row now and then. It's how you get past it that matters.'

She expected Theo to agree with her comment, but he simply looked at her and shook his head ever so slightly.

'You know that's why I love you, right? Because you see the best in everything, in everyone.'

'I don't think I saw the best in your family,' Daisy said honestly, and yet Theo leaned forward and cupped her cheeks in his hands.

'Big wedding, small wedding – I don't care. I could marry you in a castle or a barn, and I would still be the happiest man on earth,' Theo said.

'You say that like barns are a cheap alternative,' Daisy said. 'I've done my research, remember? Even a barn costs—'

'Be quiet and kiss me,' Theo said.

A minute or two later, when they broke away, Daisy could feel a familiar tightness in her face from the smile that continued to stretch her cheeks, though as her eyes met Theo's, she remembered something, and the feeling of bliss faded by a fraction.

'I guess I should go and check on Mum,' she said.

'You don't have to. She's a grown woman, and from what you said about growing up, it's not the first time she's reacted like this.'

It was true. It felt like every other month of Daisy's teen years, her mum was going through some dastardly breakup or another. But she had been with Nick a long time. This wasn't like that.

'I should go,' Daisy repeated.

'Okay, just remember that you're her child, right?'

Daisy tilted her head to the side. 'What's that meant to mean?'

'It means that your weekend wasn't as easy as we'd hoped it

would be. And you've just got engaged. You have things that you probably want and need to talk to her about too, and I don't want your mum to overshadow that.'

Daisy couldn't explain why his words made her feel so tense. Something about the way Theo was speaking reminded her of the night before. Like he was trying to put words into her mouth. Or at least thoughts into her head.

'She's obviously upset, Theo. Neither of us has any idea what happened between her and Nick. Why are you assuming that she's to blame?'

'I wasn't saying she was, I was just... It doesn't matter.'

'It obviously does, or you wouldn't have brought it up.' Daisy could feel the edge to her voice, but she wasn't prepared to leave the boat with things hanging half-said between them. 'What is it you wanted to say?'

Theo's lips twitched and his Adam's apple bobbed visibly up and down as he swallowed. 'Daisy, I think the world of your mum, you know I do, but she tends to make things about her. She doesn't always see when you need her fully.'

'That's not true.'

'Well, maybe it just looks like that to me, but when you inherited the boat and you found out she'd been lying to you, it became all about her, right? About how she couldn't cope with you being upset with her. She turned up at your work. That's what you told me.'

Daisy could feel her temperature rising, the anger within her starting to bubble. 'She had a lot of issues when I was born—'

'I'm not saying she didn't. But even when you got everything sorted, she refused to come on the *September Rose* for months and months.'

'And then she came on a massive trip with me, so that I could come and see you,' Daisy reminded him.

'I know. You're right. But she also used that moment to give you all the paintings from your dad.'

'Because I'd lost the ones from Yvonne. She knew I was upset.'

'But you wouldn't have been so upset had your mother not kept those others from you for your entire life. Do you not see that?' Theo paused and drew in a long breath, which he let out as a trembling sigh. 'Forget it. I shouldn't have said anything.'

Silence began to form, but as easy as it sounded, simply forgetting wasn't something Daisy could do at that moment.

'I'm all she's got. Maybe she leans on me more than other people's parents do, but it's always been just us. That's it. She's not had anyone else she can talk to the same way.'

Daisy had thought that point alone would be enough for Theo to drop the matter, but instead, he seemed even more incensed.

'But don't you see that's what I'm saying? You're her daughter. You shouldn't have to be dealing with her breakup issue now, and you certainly shouldn't have been dealing with them when you were growing up. That was wrong of her to put you through that.'

'You're really questioning my mother's parenting skills after the way your mum treated me?'

'I'm not questioning her parenting,' Theo tried, but Daisy wasn't having any of it.

'Yes. Yes, you are. That's exactly what you're doing.'

It was there again. That tension in her jaw. That tremble in her legs as they prepared for a fight or flight response, and once again, she knew exactly which it was going to be.

Daisy swivelled on her heel.

'Come on, Johnny,' she said. 'You can sleep on my boat tonight.'

'Daisy?' Theo tried, but Daisy was already out of the boat, the collie trotting fast behind her.

55

How could a couple who had been so perfectly in love only a week before, have more arguments in the three days since they'd got engaged than in the entire length of their relationship? It didn't make sense. Daisy's mind went over and over the last five minutes. How they had been sitting together kissing one second and then shouting at each other a moment later? She couldn't understand how it had all changed so fast, but she needed space to get her head straight. Unfortunately, space wasn't something that was currently available to her.

Holding back the tears, Daisy pushed open the door to the *September Rose* and found her mother sitting on the sofa, a half-empty bottle of wine on the coffee table as she ate from a large tub of ice cream that she'd raided from Daisy's freezer.

'You're going to have to share that,' Daisy said, heading straight to the kitchen to grab a spoon. She slammed the door shut, and a moment later dropped onto the sofa and took the tub from her mother. 'So,' Daisy said, digging deep so she could get to the chunks of caramel and chocolate chips hidden in the ice cream. 'What happened between you and Nicholas?'

Her mother let out a long sigh and reached for her wine glass. Upon finding it empty, she topped it up from the bottle and promptly swallowed several mouthfuls.

'It's just all the pushing. Like, trying to get me to go with him to Norfolk so I can get to know his children.'

'Well, that's lovely, isn't it?' Daisy said. 'And it makes sense. He knows me.'

Pippa scoffed. 'My bet is he just wants me there so I can make the food and clean up a bit while he spends all the time cuddling his new grandchild.'

'Really?' Daisy said. It was true, her mum was a great cook and her go-to form of helping people was to overload them with home-cooked food, but she couldn't imagine that was why Nicholas would have invited her.

'Did he say that to you?'

'No, of course he didn't. He says he wants me to get to know his family more, but I mean, really, it's not like he's made any effort to get to know you, is it? You live on the same canal. Having you and Theo over for a couple of barbeques doesn't take any planning when you're that close, does it?'

'Well, it's not like he's made no effort,' Daisy said, feeling the unusual urge to stick up for Nicholas. When she had first moved to Wildflower Lock, she had thought that at best, he was a miserable old man, and at worst, he was vindictive, angry and bitter. But the more she got to know him, the more her opinion had changed, and now she believed he was just very shy and guarded.

There was no denying that he had been a saviour, helping to find Yvonne's relatives and driving her back to Wildflower Lock after their failed escapades on the Thames. And then, when her mum and Daisy had arrived at their destination, he had driven all the way to Slimbridge to take Pippa back home. He also had a soft spot for Johnny, and often Daisy had thought he felt more comfortable talking to her dog than he did with her. But some people were like that, weren't they?

'So I take it you had a fight?' Daisy asked, assuming her mother's evening was a reflection of hers. And yet, surprisingly, her mother scoffed at this comment.

'No, no, Nicholas doesn't fight. He goes quiet. That was what he did, and it made my blood boil.' Pippa reached for her wine again, only to find the glass empty. Then upon seeing the bottle in the same state, she let out a slight hiss. 'He said I was being ridiculous, that he wanted me to be there because he loved me and didn't want to spend too long apart. He even said he'd do all the cooking, which we both know is ridiculous because the only thing he ever cooks is stir-in sauce.'

Daisy was struggling to follow how this had resulted in her mother storming out with her bag in her hand, so rather than beating around the bush, she asked the question.

'So what happened then?' she said.

'Well, I said that I needed space and came here.'

Daisy straightened her spine a little as she sat up.

'Sorry, so he did nothing wrong, and you just marched out?'

'Did you not hear what I just said?' Her mother rolled her eyes, although Daisy barely paid it any attention. Was Theo right? Was her mother just going through the same old routines she did with all her boyfriends when she was getting bored? Routines she really should have grown out of.

Growing up, Daisy had never been brave enough to call her mother out on her behaviour, and yet as she sat there looking at her mum who had already drunk a bottle of her wine and devoured half her ice cream, she couldn't shake the question that had formed in her head. Was Theo right?

She put the tub of ice cream down on the coffee table and turned to look at her.

'Sorry, Mum,' she said. 'But from where I'm sitting, it really looks like you're the one who's in the wrong here.'

56

Daisy waited for her mother to reply, yet all she did was stare at Daisy in silence with her jaw slack, as if in complete disbelief.

'Did you not hear what I just said?' Her mother shook her head. 'He's trying to make all these demands on me.'

'He's trying to have a grown-up relationship with you,' Daisy replied. 'That's what he's trying to do, but you don't understand that because you've never actually had one. The moment things get too tough, or you have to give a little bit more than you want to, you run.'

'Pardon?' Pippa's eyebrows rose, but Daisy couldn't stop, because she was finally letting herself speak the truth she had kept in for over half her life.

'That's what you do, Mum. You either run, or you pick complete losers with whom there's no hope of forming a proper relationship. But I don't think it's that with Nicholas. I think you're scared, and that's why you're making up all these excuses. It was exactly the same last summer when he said he'd like it if you moved closer to Wildflower Lock. You bolted then, and now he's asking for more commitment from you, and you're bolting again.'

Silence filled the boat and for a split-second, Daisy wondered if she had made a mistake. If she should have kept her thoughts to herself. But then, it was like she had said to Theo – for so long, she had been the only person her mother could lean on and Daisy owed her this. Because maybe hearing the truth would be enough for Pippa to finally stop bolting every time she got a little scared and start taking that next step in a relationship.

Daisy waited for her mother to respond. To admit that Daisy was right. But instead, her face turned a notable shade of puce.

'You don't know anything about the relationships I've been in,' she said eventually. 'You don't know a damn thing.'

The harshness of her tone caught Daisy.

'I do, actually,' Daisy said, refusing to back down. She was right and drunk or not, she was going to make sure her mother heard her. 'I know quite a lot. Because I was there for most of them. Remember Eric, the postman? He was nice. He wanted us to go on holiday with his family. You bolted then.'

'Eric was needy.' Pippa scoffed.

'It's called loving, Mum. And what about Artie, the landscape gardener?'

'Oh yes, who liked to spend weekends trawling garden centres because he couldn't switch off from his job.'

'Or because he wanted to share a part of his life that he loved with you?' Daisy countered. 'Did you ever think that could be a reason he wanted to do that with you all the time?'

With a loud huff, Pippa stood up.

'I didn't come here to be attacked, Daisy. I thought I taught you better than that.'

'I'm not attacking you. I want you to be happy. I'm trying to make you see you don't have to just give up every time things get tough. Maybe if you'd just try to compromise a little bit—'

'Compromise is just a nice way of saying no one gets what they want,' her mother scoffed. 'And thank you for the pseudo-psychology analysis of my love life, but quite frankly, I'm not in the mind to take relationship advice from someone who can't even see that their own situation is going to end in heartbreak.'

'Sorry?' Daisy tipped her head to the side, not sure she had heard her correctly. 'What did you say?'

'You heard me. I said that you and Theo are destined to be a disaster, and the fact you can't see it makes it all the more painful to watch.'

57

It was Daisy's turn to be dumbstruck. She glanced at the empty bottle of wine on the side table. She had known her mother to drink more than that over the course of an evening, but considering her mother hadn't opened the bottle until she'd boarded the *September Rose,* she had got through it unusually quickly. As if knowing what her daughter was thinking, Pippa spoke again.

'I'm sorry, Daisy, it's nothing to do with the drink. I've thought it all along. You know I have.'

'And you pick now to tell me?' Daisy asked. 'Now, when I've got engaged? After we've been together for over two years?'

'Well, it's not exactly the first time I've mentioned my concerns to you, is it?'

'Yes, yes, it is!' Daisy couldn't believe she was having this conversation, and yet her mother simply sniffed dismissively.

'I tried to tell you when you had everyone over for drinks and terrible mini quiches.'

'My engagement party, you mean?' Daisy said. She was growing more and more flabbergasted by the second. 'What perfect timing that would have been!' She drew in a long stream of air and tried to force her pulse to lower. 'I'm sorry, Mum. I obviously upset you, but you can't just start insulting my relationship with Theo because you're angry. You have never mentioned it before. As far as I was aware, you loved Theo. At least that's what you've always said.'

'Yes, I think he's a great guy,' her mother said, continuing to lift her wine glass to her lips, despite it being empty. 'But I don't think he's right for you. Not long term. I told you that when you went chasing after him down the Thames. I said it was too soon to be running after a man.'

'I wasn't running after him,' Daisy protested. She was shaking her head, struggling to believe what she was hearing. 'I was surprising him. It's something you do when you love people. And that was two years ago. If you'd really been that concerned about him, then why didn't you say anything before?'

'Well, because I thought you'd grow out of it. You know, the way people do. I mean, really Daisy, he's the first relationship you've had since you were a teen. You can't possibly think you know enough about love and relationships to get married.'

'You mean like you did when you married my dad?' Her disbelief was turning into anger. It had been years since she had been this furious at her mother, but just like then, this felt fully deserved.

'Yes,' her mum said, now standing with her hands on her hips. 'That's exactly what I'm talking about. I know what a mistake I made, thinking I was in love with your father. Or rather, thinking that what I felt for your father was enough for us to make it through the tough times. But it wasn't. It was puppy love. That euphoric feeling that makes you feel like you're on top of the world. I see the same thing with you and Theo. The pair of you are ignoring reality, tucked away here on the canal. Believe me, it's like watching the past relive itself, and it'll end in heartbreak for you, just like it did for me.'

Daisy was shaking her head, still struggling to comprehend what her mother was saying. It was the drink. It had to be. That was the reason she was saying all these things.

'You were depressed, Mum. You told me that. Several times. You left me, went to a different country because you couldn't deal with giving up on your dreams the way that having me had forced you to do. The reason your and Dad's marriage broke up had nothing to do with a lack of love or not having foresight. It was because you bolted. The way you always do. The way you're doing now. And I'm sorry, but I'm not you. I don't plan on bolting from Theo.'

'Really? Well then, you're a fool.'

'Sorry?'

'Why did you come back here tonight, Daisy? Why didn't you stay with Theo?'

'Because I was worried about you.'

'Is that right? Then what's that on your finger? That's not the ring Theo bought you.'

Daisy glanced down at her hand. She hadn't mentioned the ring situation to her mother and hadn't even been sure whether she was going to, but as she considered where to start and how much she wated Pippa to know her mother spoke again.

'Nobody changes their engagement ring without something happening. Besides, I saw it on your face the moment you walked in here and demanded the ice cream. You and Theo had a fight, right? And I'm betting it's not the first one you've had since you accepted his proposal. It's your subconscious, Daisy. It's telling you this isn't right. Face it – if you marry him, you're setting your-self up for failure, and you know it as well as I do.'

58

Daisy didn't look back. She knew Johnny was there behind her as she marched down the towpath and towards the car park and she would take him with her wherever it was she was going. She just hadn't decided where that was yet.

Her first urge had been to kick her mother out of the *September Rose,* but then what? Her mum had drunk an entire bottle of her wine and likely a fair bit more before she had left Nicholas's. There was no way she was in a fit state to drive. And Daisy couldn't go back to Theo's. The fact that he had been right about her mother didn't make Daisy feel any better. If anything, it made her feel madder for not having noticed before. Going from one argument to another was not what she wanted, and that was what she knew would happen if she returned to the *Narrow Escape.* What she wanted was a safe place, a person she could talk to without fear or judgement, and so, as she opened the back of the car and clipped Johnny in, she decided she was going to London.

Rush hour had been and gone and so Daisy drove into the city at a near record speed. Her one aim was to get away from Wildflower Lock, but it was only when she reached the multi-story car park opposite Bex's apartment block she realised there was a problem.

'Come on, and be good,' Daisy said as she hurried Johnny along on his lead. 'I don't think she's meant to have dogs here.'

Daisy pressed the buzzer to Bex's apartment, using her body to block Johnny from the road, in case there were any nosy neighbours, ready to accost her for bringing an animal into the building. She should have rung, she realised. She should have at least checked that Bex was home. Perhaps after a weekend on the boat, she had decided she wanted to go out for a bit of culture or city life, or to spend some time with whichever boyfriend she was seeing at the moment. Daisy pressed again, while simultaneously reaching for her phone to make the call she should have made an hour before. She had just swiped the screen when there was a loud buzz and crackle through the intercom.

'Hello?' Bex's voice rattled through the line.

'Bex?' Daisy couldn't stop the trembling in her voice, and once it started, there was no stopping it. All the tears she had stored up from the disastrous weekend and now the fight with her mother were bubbling to the surface, and there was nothing she could do. By her feet, Johnny was whining, pushing his body against her legs as he tried to comfort her, but it was no good.

'Daisy, is that you?'

'Bex?' Daisy's voice stuttered as she fought the tears that were rising through her throat. 'Can I come up?'

'Of course you can. What is it? What's wrong?'

The air caught in Daisy's lungs, and it was getting harder and harder to breathe, and yet she choked out the one word that summed up how she felt.

'Everything,' she said. 'Everything is wrong.'

59

Bex didn't have any wine or beer in, but Daisy didn't care. She didn't feel like a drink, anyway. She didn't feel like anything other than curling up and crying herself to sleep. It must have been obvious how terrible she looked because although she flinched a little, Bex didn't say anything as Johnny jumped up on the sofa next to her and placed his head on Daisy's lap. In fact, the only thing she'd said about Johnny so far was that she wasn't meant to have dogs in the building, so he'd need to be quiet. Thankfully, she hadn't told Daisy they needed to leave.

'I can't believe your mother said that,' Bex said, letting out a sigh. 'I love Pippa, you know I do, but she has some funny ideas about parenting. Claire and I have said it before. She's always gone for the friend route, not the mother one. I mean, letting you drop out of art college after one term is a perfect example.'

'I know,' Daisy said, glancing at her phone, although the screen was black. She'd had three missed called so far from her mother and two from Theo, so she'd switched her phone off altogether. She would speak to them when she was ready and she wouldn't be pestered into deciding when that was. 'But the thing is, do you think she's right?'

'What?' Bex's face scrunched up so much, it became a mass of wrinkles. 'About you and Theo being destined to fail? Absolutely not. It's clear that you adore each other.'

'But that's not always enough, is it? I mean, you hear it all the time, that love isn't enough, right? And this weekend has been a disaster from start to finish.'

'That's not true,' Bex said. 'The hotel was amazing. You had a great time there.'

Daisy let out a long sigh. 'I know, but that seems kind of insignificant compared to the rest of it. Maybe it was a sign. It's clear his parents don't approve of the match either. You'd think at least one set of parents would think it was a good idea.'

'Maybe, but it's not your mum or Theo's parents who are getting married, is it? It's you guys. Look, you just need to put this behind you. Think of your engagement. It was perfect.'

'A perfect five minutes when he proposed, you mean? It's not real life. I don't know...'

Daisy slowly stroked Johnny along his back before picking up her glass of water, although she didn't bother taking a sip. Instead, she just stared at it for a moment before letting out a sigh.

'I just keep thinking how she's right. At least in one sense. What do I know of real relationships? Puppy love and Theo. That's all I've had.'

'And Christian?' Bex offered, although Daisy scowled in response.

'I can't count that as a relationship. If I did, it's definitely a very failed one. Maybe I need to know more about that kind of thing before I actually commit to spending the rest of my life with a person. Take a leaf out of your book.'

'Out of my book?' Bex said, her scoff turning into a laugh. 'Now you can't be serious.'

'Why not?' Daisy questioned. 'You've dated plenty of guys. You know exactly what you're looking for, and you refuse to settle.'

'You can't possibly think of Theo as settling?' Bex said.

'I fell for the guy with the boat next to mine. That's not exactly spreading my wings and seeing what's out there, is it?' A heaviness had formed in her chest.

'Why do you think you have to travel the world or kiss a hundred frogs to find your prince?' Bex said, her expression still confused. 'If I had a guy look at me the way Theo looks at you...' She let the rest of her sentence drift off before she shook her head. 'I don't have high standards, Daisy. I have impossible standards.'

Daisy frowned. 'That's not true.'

'Yes, yes, it is. And my parents are partly to blame, too.'

'Your parents?' Daisy said, not sure she was following. 'Your parents are the most in-love couple I've ever known.'

'Exactly, and every man I meet, I'm comparing to them and their relationship. I don't go into it wondering if we might have adventures together or whether they might pull me out of my comfort zone. Instead, I nit-pick everything they do. If they eat too loudly, they're out. If they laugh at things I find unfunny, they're out. I'm too busy thinking about how annoying each foible is going to be after twenty or thirty years that I never get to the one-year mark. That's not a way to go into a relationship.'

'Maybe,' Daisy replied, though it didn't help her situation at all. Sure, she and Theo both had foibles, and mostly she found them endearing. But was that just naivety? After all, what was the possibility that her soulmate would have the mooring next to hers? If soulmates even existed. He had been there, convenient, and of course she loved him. But then, she reasoned, surely if you spent time with anyone who was as kind and fun as Theo, most people would fall in love with them in some sense or another. Was that really a reason to get married?

'Do you want me to make up the sofa bed, or would you rather crash in my bed with me?' Bex said, pulling Daisy from her thoughts.

'I'll stay here,' Daisy said. 'I'm not sure what time I'll get up in the morning.'

'Well, I wouldn't rush. According to the forecast, it's going to be heavy showers all day tomorrow.'

Rain. Daisy let out a sad chuckle. It was coming to something that rain felt like a good thing in her life.

60

Bex had been right about the rain and while that would have normally allowed Daisy the luxury of a lie-in, the fact she had Johnny with her derailed that plan.

Thinking about it objectively, bringing Johnny hadn't been her wisest decision. Not only was he not allowed in the building, but he was used to being let out first thing in the morning when Daisy moved from Theo's and headed over to the *September Rose* to start baking for the day. As such, he wasn't content just to lie around. An added complication to his early-morning walk was that he would normally have his first feed of the day then too, and Daisy hadn't brought any dog food with her.

'Come on then, and be quiet,' Daisy said as she slipped on her shoes and tied Johnny's lead to his collar, ready to take him outside. 'Just no barking, all right? I don't want Bex to get in trouble for me bringing you here.'

Bex's apartment was on the seventh floor, and normally Daisy used the lift, but the night before, with Johnny in tow, she had taken the stairs. She was aware there were probably cameras in the stairwell too, but it seemed like the right thing to do, and that morning, she felt the same. Getting in the lift with a dog in an apartment block where they were banned didn't feel right. So Daisy pushed open the heavy door into the stairwell and led Johnny down.

The cool air brushed her arms as she made her way down to the sixth floor. It hadn't seemed that far the night before, probably because she was too busy sobbing while Bex comforted her. But when she was three flights down, it already felt like she had been going forever. The last thing she wanted was for Johnny to decide he couldn't make it all the way outside and relieve himself on the steps, so she picked up her pace. She had just reached the second floor and was about to start her last flight of stairs when the door swung open.

'Hey!' Daisy said, jumping out of the way, although she wasn't fast enough. While avoiding being hit full on, the edge of the door caught the top of her arm, scraping it. Yelping, she jumped out of the way. 'Watch what you're doing!' she said.

The open door revealed a man with sandy-coloured hair wearing sports clothing, staring straight at her.

'Sorry,' he said. 'There's not normally anyone in here at this time.'

'Well, there is now,' Daisy said, rubbing the patch of her arm where the door had scraped the skin. Removing her hand revealed an impressive graze – the type she hadn't had since falling off her bike when she was younger.

'I'm so sorry,' the man said, still blocking the doorway and corridor behind him. 'I've got some antiseptic wipes in my apartment if you—' He stopped, his gaze moving from Daisy to Johnny, who had shifted behind her legs, although not well enough to remain hidden. Heat flooded through her. The man was bound to ask where she was going, and Daisy was going to have to tell the truth – that she was just visiting a friend. But she would have to lie about which flat that friend lived in. There was no way Daisy wanted to get Bex in trouble for this.

Though rather than calling her out for breaking the rules, the man laughed heartily. It was a great laugh that lit up his face and made him look substantially younger, though Daisy was still struggling to understand why he was responding in such a manner when he stepped to the side. There behind him was a fluffy Labrador retriever.

'I guess we're both up early for the same reason,' he chuckled.

61

Daisy and the man took the last flight of stairs together, with the dogs walking alongside, matching their strides perfectly.

'So you actually live here, with a dog?' Daisy said, struggling to believe that he could keep the large Labrador a secret.

'I know. I'm a rebel, right?' the guy said with a wink and a smile that Daisy couldn't help but reciprocate.

'And no one knows?'

'Well, the good thing about a larger dog is that they don't yap away like smaller ones do.'

'Still?'

The man cocked his head and offered Daisy another of his flirtatious smiles. 'A lot of people know, and there was a bit of backlash at the beginning, but as soon as I told them Bruno's story, they understood, didn't they, buster?'

The dog cocked his head towards the pair of them. He had obviously heard his name, but there was something about the way he looked at his owner that made Daisy feel like he knew exactly what they were talking about.

'What's his story?' she asked, already feeling invested in the life of this dog.

'Well.' The man let out a sigh. 'A lot of it we don't know. But he turned up at Battersea Dogs Home five years ago in an absolute state. Mites, fleas, practically no fur on him. He was a mess, apparently. I've seen a couple of photos, and honestly, it would bring you to tears. Poor guy.'

'Was he not chipped?' Daisy said, thinking of her own experience with finding Johnny. Dogs are meant to be chipped so the owners can be found if the animals became lost. Only Johnny wasn't, and the way the man was shaking his head implied that was the same for Bruno.

'Nope. Nothing on him.'

'So you adopted him?' Daisy asked, assuming this was the next logical step in the story. Only the man shook his head.

'No, not that time. Someone else did. An elderly man. He'd just lost his own dog and his wife a couple of years before and needed someone to fill the house. And Bruno did that perfectly, didn't you, boy?'

Daisy had a horrible feeling that she knew where the story was going and part of her wanted to tell the man to stop. She didn't need to hear it. She didn't want to. But she knew that wasn't the way life worked. You didn't get to fast forward the sad bits, just to skip to the happy ending.

'So what happened?' she said.

'Well, they had a couple of good years together, and then one night, the man got sick. I'm not sure exactly what happened. I think it was a heart attack, but I could be wrong. That's just me filling in blanks from what I've heard.'

'And then?' Daisy realised how impatient she sounded, but the story was coming in dribs and drabs, and while it obviously had a happy ending, she still wanted to hear how Bruno had ended up there in the stairwell with her, sniffing Johnny and wagging his tail.

'Well, when the ambulance came, he was left in the flat. That's what I know. They reckon it must have been a week or longer, but bless him, he didn't make a sound. Not even a whimper. Just helped himself to food from the bag of biscuits, although that ran out too.'

'So he was just alone in the house for a week?'

'Yup, feeling like he'd been abandoned again.'

'Oh God.' Daisy's heart ached for this poor animal. She had seen from Johnny how much love dogs had to give. How trusting and trusted they could be. Of course, she knew they weren't all like that. They were like humans; they all had their own flaws and foibles, but she couldn't imagine any animal ever deserving to suffer what Bruno had gone through, losing a home not once, but twice. 'So who found him?'

'The family, when they came to clear out the house. He didn't have any children, so it was a niece and nephew who came to sort out all the belongings. They didn't see him that often – it must have been a couple of years. They had no idea he'd even got Bruno. So he ended up back at Battersea Dogs Home. One of the volunteers knew exactly who she was looking at and wanted to find him a home where he would never be left again.'

'Wow, and so what? You were just looking for a pet?'

'No, I absolutely wasn't. But the volunteer was my baby sister, and she did her best guilt trip on me. We'd always had dogs growing up and I'd said I'd get one as soon as I got a place of my own. Of course, I hadn't anticipated being in an apartment. It wasn't the building rules that worried me. I was just worried for him, you know, with me not having a garden or anything. But she promised he was used to such rubbish conditions and that as long as he was walked a fair distance each day, he wouldn't mind it. And it's not as if my apartment is small.'

It was a valid point, Daisy thought. Bex's flat was bigger than the *September Rose* by quite some way.

'How long ago was that?' she asked.

'Four years ago. Longest relationship I've ever had, right, Bruno?' At this, the man let out a brief chuckle that faded as he looked at Daisy. A flood of embarrassment rushed to her cheeks, though she wasn't entirely sure why. Her throat had also become inexplicably dry, and she was unusually aware of her heart drumming behind her ribs.

'Well, we're on the ground floor,' she said. The comment probably wasn't necessary given that the man could see just as well as she could, but she needed to break the silence she could feel forming. Yet despite the door to the foyer being right in front of them, neither Daisy nor the man moved.

'I should—'

'You should—'

'Sorry.'

'Sorry.'

Everything the pair said was simultaneous, as were the red hues that coloured their cheeks. Daisy waited, wondering if the man was going to speak again. When it didn't look like he was, she started.

'I was just going to say that I need to get this guy out to stretch his legs.'

'Sure, and I was going to suggest that if it's all right with you, you could join us. We have a pretty standard loop we do. It has nice parks and some good views of the river too.'

Daisy looked down at the pair of dogs and then at the man. Was walking her dog with a person wrong? She wouldn't have batted an eyelid if it was a woman asking her to join them, so why did it matter if it was a young and attractive man?

'You're in running gear,' she said, suddenly grateful she could say something that wasn't outright turning him down. Because as little as she knew about him, that wasn't something she wanted to do.

'I am, but I really didn't want to go for a run. In fact, Bruno had to drag me out the door. I was dreading this morning's walk, but now I'm kind of looking forward to it. Assuming I have some company, that is.'

A smile followed. The type of smile that made Daisy's stomach flutter, even though she really didn't want it to.

'Well, Johnny does need a walk,' she said.

'Great,' the guy said, before stretching out his hand. 'I'm Ezra, by the way.'

'Daisy.'

62

The weather was grey and miserable. It was the type of day that Daisy normally had to drag herself out of bed for, particularly as there would be no need to open up the shop early. Johnny was the only reason she would get up at all, and even then she would give him the shortest walk possible in the hope that the weather would clear later, or that he would get a decent walk while he was out at work with Theo. But even though the rain pelted down and she constantly stepped in puddles, as she walked beside Ezra, chatting away, it didn't seem that bad.

'So you just found him?' Ezra said. They had now moved on to talking about Johnny's arrival in Daisy's life.

'Or he found me,' she replied. 'We're not exactly sure.'

'And you took him with you? Just like that. That's incredible.'

'Well, it wasn't quite that simple.' Daisy had already told Ezra about taking Johnny to the vets and trying to find his owners, but it was true – those parts felt insignificant compared to how much time they had spent together now.

'You should write a book about it,' Ezra said. 'I think it would make an awesome story. People love that type of thing, don't they? You know, that fortitude of spirit.'

'Maybe,' Daisy replied. 'I'm not much of a writer, though. And I'm not sure I have the time. Not with everything else. The business and such.'

'I just love it,' Ezra said, a broad smile lighting up his face. 'I love the way you talk about your life. And the fact that Johnny just lives with you on the canal boat that you've turned into a coffee shop. You know, I'll have to come and visit one day. To see Johnny, that is.'

'That would be nice,' Daisy said. 'Although Johnny doesn't spend the day in the coffee shop. He goes out to work with my boyfriend Theo in his van.' It wasn't until his name passed Daisy's lips that she realised she hadn't mentioned Theo at all. But it wasn't as if she had deliberately been avoiding him. Was it?

'You have a boyfriend,' Ezra said, eyebrows rising. 'That's a shame. Bruno was already getting quite attached.' He glanced ahead of him, to where Johnny and Bruno were walking side by side, so close together they kept bumping into one another as their tails beat furiously.

'Yes, they do seem to get on incredibly well,' Daisy said. Taking on a dog where you had no idea of its history was always going to be a risk, but Johnny had been incredible. No nips, no growls – nothing but the occasional bark. Still, she wasn't sure if her comment was entirely about the dogs.

'So this boyfriend of yours, he lives on the canal too?'

'He does,' Daisy replied. She wasn't sure why she called Theo her boyfriend rather than fiancé, other than it didn't feel right to change and suddenly start referring to him differently.

'Ah, just my luck, right?' Ezra said with a shake of his head. 'I meet the girl of my dreams and she's taken. I should have known my week could never start that well.'

It didn't matter how cold the rain was, it didn't stop the heat rising through Daisy's body.

'Oh, I don't think I'd be your ideal woman,' she said, trying to alleviate some of the tension that was building between them. 'I'm pretty average.'

'Really? Loves dogs, independent, creative, and absolutely stunning. Trust me, Daisy, you are anything but average.'

63

A large lump filled Daisy's throat, and she couldn't swallow it down. Instead, her heart was racing as Ezra stared straight at her. It was the first time she'd noticed how dark his eyes were. Their deep brown was so intense, she could barely see the irises from the pupils even though she was looking intently. That was the instant Daisy realised she was staring back at him. She was causing this moment between them too. And it was definitely a moment.

Ezra had called her stunning. Anything but average. No make-up on, no effort made. Nothing but conversation between two strangers, not that they felt like strangers now. Of course, it could have been a false compliment, an attempt at flattery, but she didn't think it was. Something about the sadness when he said it made her feel like it was the truth.

After several attempts to clear her throat, Daisy finally forced a sound out.

'Who says I'm creative?' she said, trying to distract from the last parts of his statement.

'You are, right?' Ezra replied, the eye contact now broken as they carried on walking. 'I don't know, I get that feeling from you. Like you'd need an outlet for the business and the stress of it. Maybe playing an instrument? Singing?'

At this, Daisy could help but laugh. 'Oh, trust me, you don't want to hear me sing. But you're right. I'm a painter. I paint.'

'See, I knew it. Perfect girl and taken.'

Silence swelled around them. Rain was splashing on the pavement as boats moved up and down the Thames. Daisy didn't think she'd ever be able to look at the river again without remembering her own trip on there. Her own trip to see Theo, the man she loved.

'I should get back,' Daisy said, breaking the silence that had already settled. 'Bex will wonder where I've got to. And I somehow need to get this guy dried off or she's never going to let me into her flat.'

'I've got loads of dog towels at mine. You can dry him off there before you go up to your friend's, if it helps?'

Daisy contemplated the offer. She'd had such a great morning talking to him, but there was no denying the awkwardness that followed his words, and Daisy couldn't help but feel a pang of guilt. If she'd mentioned Theo at the beginning of the walk, then they could have enjoyed all the same conversations without Ezra getting the wrong idea. But then maybe that had been the point, subconsciously at least. Maybe she'd wanted him to think she was single. Not because she had any intention of cheating on Theo, just because... just because... She wasn't sure what the because was.

'I'm sorry, I ruined things, didn't I?' This time, Ezra was the one to break the silence. 'Ignore me, please. I'm just in a melancholy mood, that's all. I shouldn't have put that on you.'

'Melancholy?' Daisy said. 'You don't seem it to me.'

'No, well, you kind of brought me out of it. Truth is, today is the one-year anniversary since my fiancée decided she didn't want to marry me. In fact, she didn't want to be with me at all.'

'Oh, wow, I'm so sorry,' Daisy said, not sure what other reaction she could give.

Ezra nodded and offered her a small smile in response.

'I know this isn't what you want to hear either, but I was planning on taking myself for a run in the rain, you know, just to complete the stereotype of the sad, lonely, heartbroken man. And then I opened the stairwell door, and you were there. And I guess... I guess... I thought fate was throwing me a bone, so to speak. But sorry, I've made you feel awkward, and I really didn't want to do that. Honestly, you've made this morning so much better than I thought it was going to be.'

'I've liked it too,' Daisy said. 'It's been good. I think with my life on the canal, it can all get a bit claustrophobic. It's nice to talk to someone different. Get a different outlook on life now and then.'

'I know exactly what you mean.'

Daisy glanced again at Johnny. He was wearing his spare wet-weather coat that had been in the car when she'd driven to Bex's, but it didn't stop his head, legs and tail from dripping.

'Does that offer of a towel still apply?' she said.

A smile twisted on the corner of Ezra lips.

'Of course it does.'

Daisy went to thank him, only to pause. There was another question she probably needed to ask him and there didn't seem like any point in waiting.

'I don't suppose I could pinch some of your dog food too, could I?'

'Jeez, break my heart then steal my dog food.' Ezra grinned.
'I'm sure I can manage that for Johnny.'

'For Johnny?' Daisy smiled back.

'Exactly.'

64

Even after several minutes with a towel, Johnny still wasn't bone dry, but his feet were clean, his fur was no longer dripping and he'd eaten a large bowl of Bruno's dog food which would be more than enough to see him through the morning.

'Thank you,' Daisy said, as she prepared to leave Ezra's apartment.

'It was a pleasure, honestly,' Ezra replied. 'Who knows? Maybe I'll see you again. And Johnny, too. You know him and Bruno are lifelong friends now.'

Daisy grinned as she opened the door and stepped across the corridor to the stairwell.

'I know. I'm sure he'll be pestering me for another playdate as soon as we leave. And don't worry, your secret about having a dog here is safe with me.'

A cheeky smile curled at the corner of Ezra's lips. It was the exact smile that had made her stomach flutter earlier and it was doing the same again, though she was trying her hardest to ignore it.

'I'll be honest with you, I don't think it's much of a secret,' he said. 'See you later, Daisy and Johnny.'

As if knowing what response was expected, Johnny offered a single bark before he and Daisy headed up the stairs towards Bex's flat.

It was only when she reached the seventh floor that Daisy realised she still hadn't taken her phone with her. In fact, she hadn't even turned it back on since she'd had enough of all the missed calls the night before. At some point, she knew she'd have to deal with a barrage of messages from Theo and her mother, but she wanted to make sure she had a cup of tea in her hand before she did that.

With Johnny sitting by her heel, she knocked on Bex's front door.

Immediately, it swung open.

'Where've you been? You've been gone for ages,' Bex said.

'I took Johnny for a walk and I've been downstairs with your neighbour since I got back.'

'What? Who?'

'Ezra. He lives on the second floor. You must know him. You have a radar for hot guys. And he is definitely hot. He's also unbelievably lovely and has the most gorgeous dog, Bruno. I can't believe you don't know who he is.'

Bex's normal response upon hearing about a good-looking man was to ask as many questions as possible to establish whether he would be suitable dating material. Especially one who lived so close to her. But rather than doing that, her face paled.

'Daisy,' she said.

'What? I think he's your type. I mean, he said I was stunning and his ideal woman, but—'

'Daisy,' Bex said again, this time more firmly. Her head

remained forward, but her eyes shifted to the side as if she was implying there was something inside the apartment she wanted Daisy to see.

A second later, Daisy realised exactly what Bex was trying to tell her. Theo was there. Theo was there, and he had heard every word Daisy had just said.

65

Silence threatened to suffocate Daisy, and she knew she had to say something, yet her mind was completely blank. Had she said anything incriminating? She had said that Ezra was good-looking, sure, but she'd also mentioned the dog, right? Surely they knew the only reason she'd gone to Ezra's flat was because of the dogs.

'Well, it's time I left for work,' Bex said. 'You guys stay as long as you like. Just close the door when you leave.' She slipped past Daisy, squeezing her hand briefly as she went.

A large weight filled Daisy's stomach as she and Theo were left alone. Almost alone. Johnny wasted no time as he raced over to Theo. However, instead of giving Johnny his usual fuss and affection, Theo remained entirely still, continuing to stare at Daisy.

'I tried ringing you,' he said.

'I know. I turned my phone off.'

'Because you were with this guy, Ezra?'

Daisy raised her eyebrows. 'No, I turned my phone off last

night because I needed some space. That's why I'm here, because I needed some space.'

'I get that,' Theo said, nodding his head. 'But I thought that meant going to the *September Rose*. Then I went there this morning to apologise and found out you hadn't even spent the night there. And then I tried ringing you and it kept going straight to answerphone. I had to call in sick to work to find you.'

A flicker of guilt sparked in Daisy, but it extinguished itself almost immediately.

'You didn't have to come looking for me at all, Theo. I'm an adult. I'm fine.'

'With this Ezra guy?'

Daisy bit her lower lip. She could sense the argument brewing, though she wasn't sure what its focus would be or how to stop it – or if she even wanted to.

'I was walking the dog with him. He had a dog to walk as well.'

'And that ended with you in his flat?'

'Yes, because he had towels to dry the dogs. And food too. He's a dog owner, unlike Bex, and I didn't want to track mud through her flat and I didn't want our dog to go hungry either.'

'You could have just borrowed one of his dog towels and a bowl of food.'

'Did you hear what I said?' Daisy replied. 'I didn't want to bring a dripping wet dog into my friend's apartment when she's not meant to have pets in here. Why are we even talking about this?'

'Well, you're the one who brought him up.' A muscle twitched along Theo's jawline. '"Gorgeous," that's what you said, wasn't it? No, sorry, I remember now. It was "hot." "Definitely hot." And how did he describe you?'

'I'm sorry, Theo, but is this you being jealous? Am I supposed to feel guilty about this when you spent the night after our engagement chatting to your ex-girlfriend – or was it ex-fiancée? I can't quite remember, because she didn't take the ring you gave me, did she?'

Daisy knew her words were harsh, but she wasn't going to let Theo accuse her of something she hadn't done. She wasn't accepting his passive-aggressive behaviour.

'Your mum said you had a fight,' Theo said abruptly, shifting the conversation in a way Daisy suspected was an attempt to prevent her from getting mad at him.

'Yes, we did.' She folded her arms across her chest.

'Do you want to tell me what it was about?'

'Well, not that you probably want to hear it, but she doesn't think we should get married. She thinks I lack experience in relationships and that it'll all end miserably.'

At this, Theo looked suitably stunned. His jaw dropped. 'Wow. What did you tell her? You told her that's nonsense, right?'

'What do you think I told her? No, I said I thought she was completely right and that I'd call off the engagement right away.'

His eyes widened. 'Seriously? You didn't?'

'No, of course I didn't! For crying out loud, Theo, if you don't trust that I'd stand up for us and our relationship, and if you don't trust that I can't go into an attractive man's house without – what? Undressing him? – then maybe my mum is right. Maybe we seriously need to rethink this relationship.'

'Do you mean the engagement?' Theo asked, looking at her with a pained expression on his face.

Daisy shook her head.

'No, Theo, I mean the relationship.'

66

'I think it's over.'

Those were the first words Daisy said to Bex when she walked into the apartment several hours later. Theo had already gone and had taken Johnny with him, leaving her alone with her thoughts, which were, quite frankly, a mess.

For a while, she had considered going down to Ezra's just so that she could cuddle Bruno and feel a little less alone, but using a man who had already said he was attracted to you for their dog wasn't exactly the right thing to do, and she knew that. And so she sat there, alone, in silence until Bex returned.

'What do you mean, it's over?' Bex said, dropping to her knees beside her. Daisy hadn't even thought about what time of day it was, or that Bex had probably come home during her lunch break to check on her.

'Me and Theo, I think we're over.'

'Don't be silly. You can't be.'

'I think we are.'

Bex tilted her head to the side as she looked up at Daisy. It was like she didn't believe anything she was saying. 'But he proposed. He proposed four days ago, Daisy.'

'I know. And I wish to God he hadn't. I wish we could go back to the way things were before.' At some point during the morning, Daisy knew she had cried, but she wasn't sure when or how long the tears had lasted. Now, though, her throat felt red raw. As if it was all she had done.

'Well, what happened?' Bex asked, not wanting to accept 'it's over' as an answer.

'What didn't happen? My mum thinks it's a terrible idea. His family despise me. We have vastly different financial situations. He thinks a small wedding is sixty people, and we don't even know if we want the same things in life, like children. That's a big deal. And then you need to add to that the fact he doesn't even trust me.'

This was the one that stung the most. This was the thing she couldn't get her head around. Though Bex merely shook her head.

'That's not true. He does. Theo trusts you implicitly.'

'You didn't hear what he said.'

'Well... in his defence, you did come into my flat saying that you'd spent the morning having fun downstairs with my hot neighbour.'

'That was not how I worded it,' Daisy said indignantly.

'It was pretty close.'

Daisy pouted. 'Fine, but did you take that to mean I'd cheated on Theo?'

'No, of course I didn't,' Bex said, shaking her head. 'But I knew where you were. I hadn't spent the morning looking for you. Look, can I be honest with you?'

With a shake of her head, Daisy drew a deep breath in.

Honesty came without question in their friendship, so the fact that Bex had to clarify it didn't make her feel good.

'Of course you can,' Daisy said.

'I think you're putting too much pressure on the idea of getting married. You said you want to go back to how things were, so why don't you do that? Forget about the engagement. Just go back to how things were before.'

'But we can't, can we? It's not possible. The truth is out there now. There's no real future for us. Not with the way our families feel.'

'Your families don't matter in this. That's the whole point of getting married, isn't it? That you get to choose the family you want to spend your life with, rather than having to survive the one you were born into?'

At this, Daisy let out a sad chuckle. She'd said something remarkably similar to Theo the night he proposed, and it had felt so true at the time.

'Maybe, but it doesn't change how I don't know what I want in terms of children while he's dead-set. It doesn't feel right stringing him along if I might decide I never want them. Looking at it objectively, I can see why our parents don't think it's going to work.'

'Why are you looking at it objectively?' Bex asked. 'This is love. It's the least objective thing there is out there. Please don't do this to yourself. I meant what I said last night. If I had found my Theo, I would have settled down years ago.'

'Maybe,' Daisy said. She couldn't even look her friend in the eye any more. 'Or maybe you're just wise enough to see that it's nothing more than an illusion. And we had a good run. That's for sure. But I think it's better this way. It's better now, before we're any more committed. This way, he's got time to find someone who can give him what he really wants in life.'

67

Heartbreak was such a funny term, in Daisy's mind at least. Everyone who had ever said they were heartbroken knew that it wasn't a physical ailment. Their heart was perfectly intact, pumping blood through their body the way it was meant to. And yet it didn't feel that way. It felt like with every breath, sharp needles were puncturing your chest. As though every muscle behind your ribs had been ripped to shreds and would never repair. And for Daisy, the pain extended well beyond where her heart sat. Her head pounded while waves of nausea struck at the most random times, and more than once on the journey out of London, she had to stop to pull over just to let the tears out, like that might be the solution for all this hurt she was feeling.

'You can stay here for longer,' Bex said as she walked Daisy to her car, but Daisy shook her head.

'There's no point in not facing it,' she said. 'We'll need to work out logistics. Johnny, living so close, that type of thing.'

'Okay, but you can come back at any time you want. You know that?'

'Thank you. Thank you for everything.'

Bex pulled her in for a tight hug, but even when they broke away, she held Daisy by the shoulders.

'Think on this, okay? Don't rush this decision. You can take all the time you want.'

'Only that isn't fair on him, is it?' Daisy replied. 'I get what you're saying, but it's okay. I'm going to be all right.'

As she climbed into her car and buckled the seatbelt, she wondered just how true that was.

'This is for the best,' she told herself repeatedly. 'This is to make sure it doesn't hurt even more in the future.'

Her lack of focus meant that Daisy was travelling out of the city bang on rush hour, although in some ways, she was grateful. She didn't feel so bad crying when the traffic was moving so slowly. It felt far less dangerous than crying at speed.

Hundreds of thoughts were rolling through her head as she finally turned into Wildflower Lock, though the prominent one was that she hoped her mother wasn't still in the *September Rose*. She had received several messages from her mum during the day, but she hadn't read any of them. She hadn't even opened her phone. There was no one she wanted to speak to.

Yet as she walked towards the *September Rose* and was flooded with the memory of how it looked only a few nights ago, covered in fairy lights with Theo kneeling on one knee with a ring in his hand, she knew that wasn't entirely true.

68

It was just gone nine when Daisy heard the knock on the door of the *September Rose*. Despite the urge to message Theo, she had resisted, and had spent the evening sorting out Theo's belongings. Of which there were a lot. She'd hoped to fit them all into a couple of plastic bags but had needed to dig out a large packing box too.

'Can I come in?' Theo said when she opened the door.

The sun illuminated his silhouette like he was part of an ethereal painting. Daisy's chest jolted at the sight. How she had thought Ezra was good-looking was a mystery to her. She had never been attracted to anyone the way she was with Theo. But attraction wasn't enough to make a marriage work, was it?

Unable to speak, she nodded once then stepped out of the way, giving Theo room to move into the boat. He was barely two steps in when he stopped again.

'What's this?' he said, looking at the box and bags which Daisy had piled up by the door.

'They're your belongings,' Daisy replied, her voice cracking as she spoke. 'I thought it was best to do this quickly, you know, so that we can move on. There's probably a lot more of my things at yours, you know, with all the nights I've stayed there and everything.'

The look of hurt and disbelief on his face was enough to bring tears to the back of Daisy's throat. She tried to swallow them back down, but it didn't work. A stray tear caught in the corner of her eye and trickled down her cheek.

'Why are you doing this, Daisy?' Theo said, stepping towards her.

Daisy stepped back. She couldn't let him touch her. If she did, she knew all her resolve would crumble.

'It's best in the long run,' she replied. 'I know it doesn't feel like it now, but it's easier this way. We want different things.'

'I want to make you happy,' Theo replied. 'That's all I want to do. That's all I've ever wanted to do. What is it you want that can be so different from that?'

'Please, Theo, don't make this any harder than it already is.'

Theo shook his head. Still, that same look of disbelief filled his face.

'And what about Johnny? What happens there? He just lives with me? You just forget about him? That's great for a dog who's already been abandoned once.'

The tears were streaming down Daisy's cheeks now, so hard and so fast that she couldn't stop them, but she had already thought through the Johnny issue.

'He'd have to stay living with you, of course,' Daisy replied, trying to keep her voice steady as she spoke. 'And go to work with you. But I was hoping perhaps I could just do his evening walks. You know, like we used to do together.'

'For God's sake, Daisy.' Theo's voice rose. 'I get it. I screwed up this last weekend. I said some things that weren't great, I know that, but please, you can't want to end everything because of a couple of bad days. Couples have bad days.'

'I don't want to end things,' Daisy said through her sobs. 'I love you. But we have to think about the future. You want children, lots. You're young enough to find someone to still do that with. And I... I will just figure me out. It's for the best. It is, I promise.'

For a second, she assumed Theo was going to offer more protests, try to plead with her again, but instead, he stepped back and looked at her as if he had no idea who she was. It was in that moment that his face hardened.

'You know what Heather said to me this weekend when I was congratulating her and telling her how I'd proposed to you? She said, "I guess I was wrong then. You know, I always thought she would break your heart." That's what Heather said, and I replied that you nearly did once, but you put it back together and it was forever. That's what I told her. But God, how wrong was I.'

The hardness in his expression had transformed to anger that Daisy could see simmering away beneath the surface. She stepped toward him, only to stop herself. It wasn't her place to comfort him any more.

'You broke my heart before, Daisy. You did, and I promised myself I would never be foolish enough to let you do that again. But you have. You know that? You have broken my heart in ways I didn't know it could be broken. So I hope whatever the terrifying future you envisioned was, it was bad enough to destroy everything we'd made. Goodbye, Daisy. I won't be giving you the chance to break my heart again.'

69

Daisy could hear the birds singing outside. Sunlight streamed through the gap in the curtains, and yet she rolled over, wishing she could ignore it.

'That's odd. They're normally open by now,' a voice said outside. 'Perhaps they're just running late. I'm sure we'll be able to grab a coffee on the way back.'

It wasn't the first voice she'd heard that morning wondering why the coffee shop was closed and questioning when she would open, but the truth was, Daisy didn't know when she was going to open it again. She wasn't even sure she could.

She closed her eyes, wanting to shut it all out, when a hammering on the hatch caused her to jerk upward.

'We're closed!' she yelled, before dropping back down onto her bed and staring up at the ceiling. It had been a long time since she'd slept in the *September Rose*, and after the *Narrow Escape*, the wide beam canal boat felt cavernous. Especially with an entire double bed to herself and no collie sleeping at her feet. She had always thought having Johnny in bed with them meant there wasn't enough room to sleep, but she had barely managed a couple of hours that night without rolling over and finding herself startled by the emptiness.

Reaching over to the bedside table, she picked up a glass of water and took a sip, though it did little to alleviate the headache that was throbbing behind her temples. There was something about the headache you got from crying, she remembered. It was more than just dehydration from the tears. It was like your entire body was drained. That was how it felt to her, at least.

She rolled back over, hoping to drift back to sleep, when her phone rang. Claire's name flashed up on the screen. No doubt Bex had filled her in on the events of the previous day and she was trying to check in on her. But Daisy didn't want to be checked in on. Daisy wanted to curl up until winter and then hibernate through that. She didn't want to deal with anyone. Even her best friends.

After a moment or two, the phone stopped ringing and Daisy dropped back to the bed, although her head had barely hit the pillow when a message pinged through. Again, it was Claire.

I'm at the canal. See you in five.

Daisy jolted upright, picked up her phone and hastily hit call on the number.

Claire answered on one ring.

'I knew that would get you speaking to me,' she said. Daisy could almost see the smirk on her friend's face and a pang of annoyance struck her from having fallen for such an obvious ploy. 'Now, what's going on?'

'You're not here? You're not at the lock?'

'Not yet. I'm twenty minutes away. But I *am* coming, which

means you have time to get yourself out of bed, in the shower and dressed before I get there.'

'How do you know I'm not already up and dressed?'

'I was with you through the Paul breakup, remember?' Claire replied.

A bitter laugh formed in Daisy's lungs, though before she could release it, another question struck.

'How do you know we broke up?'

While the girls were always there for one another, Daisy would have expected Bex to have given her the time to tell people about the breakup herself. Especially considering it had only just happened. That was why their friendships worked so well – they knew when to give one another space if it was needed. Calling Claire straight away didn't feel like something Bex would have done in this situation.

'Claire?' Daisy pressed.

A slight pause filled the line before Claire spoke again. 'Theo rang last night,' she said.

'He did? Why? To tell you that we'd broken up? God, what the hell.'

'He rang because he was confused, Daisy. He wanted to know if I had any idea what had caused this, but I have to say, I'm as confused as him. The last time I saw you, you were so in love. I mean, it's only four days since you said yes to marrying him.'

Why did people keep saying that to her? Daisy wanted to ask. Did they think she couldn't recall the moment herself? She knew when and what she had said yes to, but she also knew that worlds could change in the blink of an eye and that was what had happened to her.

'Look, we'll talk about it when I get to yours,' Claire said. 'Do you need me to pick anything up for you?'

Daisy shook her head before remembering they were on a voice call. 'No, I'm fine, and honestly, you don't need to come. I'm okay.'

'Yeah, right,' Claire scoffed. 'You can't lie to me, remember? I'll see you in twenty. And get dressed!'

70

Daisy had hoped that a shower would help, that the cold water would wake her up and make her see with absolute clarity that she had made the right decision. But unfortunately, it didn't. Instead, it just made all the memories clearer in her mind. The look of betrayal and disbelief in Theo's eyes. The anger that it had transformed to. Heather had been right about her. Of course she had. Heather was perfect. Beautiful, smart, a family woman who knew before she was even married what she wanted her future to be. She was the type of person Theo should end up with. Of course, Daisy had ruined that chance for him, but there were plenty of lovely people out there. Someone would be good enough for him, and he would find them, get married, have the family he dreamed of, and she would become nothing more than a distant memory. A barely significant chapter in the story of his life.

'God, you look like crap. Now tell me, what the hell is going on?' Claire wasn't normally the one to offer the hard truths to Daisy; that was Bex's job. Claire would offer the softer mothering approach instead, but at that moment, she didn't look soft at all. 'Have you lost your mind?'

'Don't you start,' Daisy groaned as she walked over to the coffee machine. She wasn't planning on opening the café that day, but that wasn't going to stop her from having several double espressos.

'I'm just trying to work out what happened,' Claire said when Daisy was sat back on the sofa. 'You two are perfect together, living your crazy lives on these boats of yours. He adores you. And you adore him. At least, I thought you did.'

'Oh, I do,' Daisy said. After all, there was no point in lying about how she felt – Claire would see straight through it. And her feelings weren't the reason she had ended things. Not directly, anyway. 'He's the best person I've ever known. But that's just me being short-sighted. I have to think about the future. I have to face facts.'

'What facts? Theo wants to marry you.' Claire's face was a crumple of confusion.

'Yeah, so much so, he didn't even think about the ring he was giving me. And I'm not saying I'm mad at that. I get why he wanted me to have it, but maybe it was a sign that neither of us wanted to consider. I mean, if he ignores something that significant, then it's not meant to be, is it?'

'Do you know how many thoughtless things Ian has done in our marriage? And by thoughtless, I mean he just didn't think? It's not malicious. Just sometimes people don't think. Do you not remember the day before our wedding when he took a friend's last-minute ticket to see Green Day because he'd booked the day off work and totally forgot it was to sort out the wedding venue?'

Daisy let out a brief chuckle. She remembered that day as clearly as if it had been the week before. Claire and Ian had booked a fairly nondescript barn for the reception and, given their budget, had opted to do everything themselves, from putting up lights and colourful bunting, to securing large, flowing drapes which hung from the ceiling. Only Ian's mishap meant Daisy and Bex were working on it until gone midnight.

'If anyone was going to read into signs as to why they shouldn't get married, then surely that would be one?' Claire said. 'I could have called it off then and there. God knows my mother wanted me to. But then think of all the years of happiness I would have missed out on.'

'But that's different,' Daisy said. 'You and Ian were born to be together. You knew that from day one. You're soulmates.'

'What does that mean?' Claire said, looking Daisy straight in the eye. 'We fell in love young and ridiculously quickly, yes. But it takes more than that to make a relationship a happy one that lasts. We both make mistakes. We're human. But any relationship, whether it's marriage or not, is about forgiveness and tolerance and compromise.'

A slight snort left Daisy's lips. 'Compromise is just a nice way of saying no one gets what they want,' she said, quoting her mother.

Claire frowned. 'I don't see it that way at all. Neither does Ian. For us, a compromise is a way we get to make sure the other person is happy. It isn't about someone losing out at all, and it doesn't have to be,' she said. 'If anything, it's the opposite. I'm happy when I can make something work that means Ian is happy too. That's what being in a relationship is about, isn't it? Wanting each other to be happy.'

Daisy recalled Theo's words to her from the night before. How he'd said that all he wanted to do was make her happy. And she felt the same way, too. She liked to do things she knew would make him smile. Like when she shut up the shop a little earlier, even though she might miss out on a few sales, because she wanted to get back and make sure the *Narrow Escape* was tidy the way he liked it. Or when he got up every weekend to work with her, even though he had a full-time job of his own, so they got to spend more time together. Making him happy was what made her happiest too.

A slight warmth began to fill her, but Daisy shook her head and forced it down. Two years wasn't that long into a relationship really, was it? And of course they'd wanted to spend so much time together, given all the months he'd lived away. But that would change, wouldn't it? The honeymoon stage would always have ended at some point. Better now than ten years down the road.

'You know what, I think I should probably open up now,' Daisy said, standing up and downing her drink in one. 'You don't want to hang around here with me. You must have more impor-tant things to do.'

'Actually,' Claire said, pushing back her shoulders and giving Daisy a look that was almost withering, 'being with you right now *is* the most important thing I have to do. And as I'm a dab hand at making cappuccinos, I'm going to stay and help, and don't you dare try to stop me.'

71

Claire stayed until after the lunchtime rush, and as much as Daisy didn't want to admit it, she was grateful. More than once during the day she suddenly welled up uncontrollably and had to excuse herself from serving. One time was when she saw an old couple walking arm in arm. She had served the pair dozens of times before and they always ordered two drinks and a cake to share, and though the drinks were always lattes, what cake they chose varied. Daisy hadn't yet learned their names, but she always felt a warmth when she saw them coming towards her. Except that day. That day, seeing them caused her stomach to drop, her chest to tighten, and a sickness to swell through her. So many times, she had imagined that they were what she and Theo would be like when they were old. She had even said so much to him.

'Although I'd have my own slice of cake,' Daisy had said when she'd told him about them a month or so before.

'I would buy you all the slices of cake you could want,' Theo had replied. 'Although it would be tough because they probably wouldn't be as good as ones you make.'

'You know you're the one who taught me to bake half the things I can do, right?' Daisy had laughed. 'And you still do them better than me, in most cases.'

'In that case, I will bake you all the cakes you want,' he'd said. And then they'd kissed. It hadn't been a passionate kiss. It had been gentle and light, the type of kiss people shared when they thought they had a lifetime of sharing kisses ahead of them.

'Are you okay if you serve these two?' Daisy had said to Claire before disappearing back into the boat without waiting for a reply. When she had reappeared at the hatch twenty minutes later with blotchy red eyes and her mascara smudged, Claire hadn't said a thing.

The second time Daisy had to excuse herself was because of a dog and his owners. A young couple was walking a spaniel puppy, but they could barely get two steps without the dog stopping and turning around to bound up at them. Its tail wagged furiously as it covered them in licks and each time, the young couple spent several minutes fussing over their dog. Daisy and Theo had talked about getting a puppy plenty of times. Company for Johnny. That was the excuse they used, although in truth, they both would have loved a little one to look after, even though they knew how much trouble it could be. Thankfully, the couple hadn't come to the coffee shop and ordered from her, but still, Daisy struggled to watch them.

'I'm going to have to head off now,' Claire said when it hit two o'clock. 'Amelia's in an after-school club, but I don't want to hit the traffic getting back.'

'Thank you,' Daisy said. 'I think you were right. Having you here was a good thing.'

'You'd do the same for me,' Claire replied, and Daisy didn't disagree. She had the best friends in the world and she would do anything she could for them. Claire reached in for a hug and

Daisy squeezed her as tightly as she could, hoping it would be enough to convey the gratitude she felt.

'Just call us, any of us,' Claire said when they broke apart. 'And maybe call Theo too. I don't think this is anything you two can't get past if you want to.'

'Thank you,' Daisy said. 'But what's happened is for the best. In the long run, at least.'

Daisy could see there were more things Claire wanted to say. Words twitching on her lips. But she held them in.

'If you say so,' she said instead. 'Speak to you later, okay?'

'Absolutely. You know I love you, right?'

'I love you too. Take care of yourself.'

A moment later, Claire was gone and the *September Rose* felt emptier than it had ever done before.

72

While Daisy had been grateful for Claire's appearance and knew she needed to ring Bex later in the evening to fill her in, there was one person Daisy couldn't cope with taking calls from, and that was her mother.

Pippa had left several messages apologising for the way she had acted on Sunday night, but so far Daisy had yet to respond to any of them. It was pride more than anything else. Daisy didn't want to have to look her mother in the eye and tell her she was right. The relationship was over. She was too immature to make it last. It was silly, really. After all, her mother had been the one who said she should end things, but something about telling her made it all the more real, and Daisy didn't want to deal with that.

Although the reality hit firmly at five thirty that evening when there was a sharp knock on her door.

When Daisy first moved into Wildflower Lock, any knock on the door would be a surprise. She didn't know many people other than Yvonne and Theo. And even though Yvonne had moved into a home, meaning she no longer popped her head around the corner to say hello, there were plenty of people who did. A young family had moved into the mooring on the other side of the bridge at the beginning of the year and, as new boat owners, Daisy would regularly find herself embroiled in conversations with them about the transition to life on the canals. In fact, she was normally their first port of call when they wanted to know something. Francis on the *Georgianna* liked to rescue animals and Daisy had gone up in her estimations substantially since she'd adopted Johnny while Elliot, the elderly woodworker, had a permanent mooring though he used his boat as a workshop rather than to live in. Then there were Kate and Nick, who made the amazing quiches and dozens of other people Daisy now considered firm acquaintances if not friends. In terms of who would knock at the door, it could be anyone, and yet something about the knock was immediately recognisable. Daisy's stomach twisted in knots. She checked her appearance in the mirror, only to decide it didn't matter that much.

The second she opened the door, Johnny bounded up at her feet. She crouched down to rub behind his ears in the place she knew he loved.

'Hey, you, are you ready to go for a walkie?' she said. The dog moved as if to lick her face, but before he could, Daisy stood up and looked at Theo. 'Thank you for bringing him over.'

'Yes, well, I needed to drop this stuff off too,' Theo gestured to the item he had placed on the stern behind him. A large suitcase. 'There're still a load more boxes at my place. I'll move them all over while you're walking him. I'll lock up and put the key through the letterbox.'

His voice was so stoic, Daisy barely recognised it.

'Oh, okay, yes, thank you.' A dense weight had filled her from the chest down. 'I hadn't expected you to get it all sorted so soon.'

'Like you said, there's no point delaying things.'

Theo turned to leave, but it was like his body was directly

connected to her heart. It was like he was pulling it out of her chest as he moved away from her.

'Theo,' Daisy called, unsure what she wanted to say, only knowing that she had to speak his name.

'What, Daisy?' He spun back around to face her. 'What do you want? Do you even know? Because you know what? We were so good. I just want you to know that. Whatever it is you think you'll find out there, there's nothing better than what we had together. You'll be disappointed, you know that, don't you? You are going to end up regretting this.'

A moment later, he was marching away. The minute she closed the door, her knees buckled. As she remained there, crumpled on the ground next to Johnny, she whispered in the dog's ear.

'It's best in the long run,' she said. 'We need to remember that, right, boy? It's better for us all in the long run.'

73

After her walk with Johnny, Daisy headed straight to the *Narrow Escape* to return him to Theo for the rest of the night. That was what their routine was going to be, and she wanted to get into it as quickly as possible, for Johnny's sake as well as hers.

Theo was already waiting on the stern, so Daisy didn't even have to go into the boat. There were no exchanges of words this time. No hard truths that he wanted her to hear. Instead, he simply took Johnny's leash and led him back inside. That was it.

Whether it was easier not speaking or not, Daisy didn't know, but when she returned to the *September Rose* to find several more bags and boxes sitting just inside the door and Theo's key to the boat in her letterbox, still attached to the little wooden keyring she'd bought him, she knew she couldn't stay in Wildflower Lock, knowing that Theo was just across the water from her. Not this soon. So twenty minutes after returning, she was back out in her car, heading towards Bex's. She had already set an alarm for the morning. She doubted she'd be in any fit state to work if she spent all night tossing and turning and didn't get any sleep, which she was certain would happen if she stayed on *the September Rose*.

Hopefully this way, sharing Bex's bed with her, she'd get a couple of hours. That was the plan at least, although when she arrived at the apartment building, it was a different face she saw waiting outside.

'Daisy?' Ezra's face lit up with a broad smile. 'I wasn't expecting to see you again so soon.'

'Hey. Hey, Bruno,' Daisy said.

Daisy took a deep breath in and forced herself to smile. She wasn't sure which was harder, looking at Bruno or looking at Ezra, but she decided to go for the former. The dog's tail wagged excitedly, although he looked behind her, as if he were searching for his friend. Reading his pet's expression, Ezra spoke.

'Where's Johnny?'

'Johnny is with my... my ex,' Daisy said. If she'd thought the word 'fiancé' was hard to say, getting the word 'ex' out felt like trying to speak with daggers in her throat.

'Ex? What happened?' Ezra asked. 'No, sorry, you don't need to answer that. It's none of my business. You're here to see your friend?'

Daisy nodded.

'Well, don't let me keep you.'

He moved as if he were going to walk away, and yet he barely reached the edge of the pavement when he stopped and turned to look at her.

'Look, I know this is probably hugely insensitive, and judging from our conversation yesterday, this is a very new thing, but can I give you my number? You don't have to message me, not anytime soon, if you don't want to. But who knows, maybe in a few weeks, you might want someone to go for a dog walk with? Or a coffee.'

He had such an open expression on his face that Daisy couldn't help but feel drawn to it. Maybe when she had been single, before Theo, it would have been an offer she would have immediately taken him up on. But a lot had changed since then.

'I tell you what,' she said. 'If that happens, I'll post my number through your door. How would that be?'

A flicker of disappointment flashed on Ezra's face, but he covered it quickly.

'I'll keep my eye out for it,' he said, throwing her a smile. 'Come on, boy, you need your walk.'

Daisy watched them for a moment before she headed inside and took the lift up to the seventh floor.

74

'I'll put in to work remotely,' Bex said, when Daisy had told her everything that had happened over the last twenty-four hours. 'Enough people do it. I can come down to Wildflower Lock, just for a week or so. Make sure you're not on your own.'

'You don't have to do that,' Daisy said, struck by just how generous her friends were.

'Well, I think I do. It's either that or you keep turning up at my flat without warning.' She let out a laugh that was clearly intended to make Daisy smile, although Daisy couldn't manage it. It felt as if the muscles had forgotten how to do that. As such, Bex's smile faded almost instantly.

'Look, it would do me some good too,' she said, adopting a more serious tone. 'I've been working way too late most nights. I only got back twenty minutes before you got here tonight. Working the weekend at the coffee shop actually felt like a break.'

'According to Amelia, that was because she did all the work,' Daisy replied. Bex chuckled and this time, Daisy felt a smile twisting on her lips. There was a strange unfamiliarity about the action. 'Thank you. I would really like that. But please don't feel like you have to stay the whole week.'

'How about we play it by ear? I'll pack some things tonight for a couple of days, then we can see how you're doing after that. And I'll need to go into the office first thing in the morning, but I can be down at the Lock with you by midday, if that's okay?'

Daisy wanted to be strong. She wanted to make out like she could do it on her own and that her heart didn't feel like it had been shattered into a thousand pieces, but it wasn't true. Having Claire visit had shown her that. She wasn't ready to be on her own just yet and at least this way she wasn't losing business, too.

'That would be good. Thank you,' she said. 'Thank you for everything.'

'That's what we're here for,' Bex replied, giving her a quick squeeze before standing up. 'Come on. I need to put clean sheets on if you're sleeping in my bed tonight.'

'Just to warn you, my alarm's set for four thirty,' Daisy said, also standing. 'I figured that will give me enough time to get back, do some baking and open the café at normal time.'

Bex's lips parted, though it took a moment for her to speak. 'Four thirty. Well, that confirms it. I am definitely staying at yours from now on.'

75

For the next three days, Daisy remained at Wildflower Lock. Bex stayed at her side the entire time, except for the hour or so in the evenings when Daisy took Johnny for a walk. From what Daisy could tell, remote working for Bex consisted of occasionally logging on to her computer, sounding very cross during online meetings, then coming in to tell Daisy how everyone was completely useless and that it would do them good to not have her in the office for a few days. For the most part, Daisy could almost believe life was carrying on as normal, except between 5.30 and 6.00 when Theo would appear outside the boat with Johnny, and the handover would occur.

'He wouldn't even look at me tonight,' Daisy said. It was Thursday evening, and the pair were sitting on the sofa drinking wine. Despite every night that week being clear and warm, Daisy had chosen to stay inside in the evenings, just to avoid bumping into anyone. As far as she was aware, everyone on the lock still thought she and Theo were a couple, and she didn't have it in her to tell them the news. Besides, she'd spent plenty of time out and about.

Daisy had taken Johnny on an extra-long walk that day, as they hadn't discussed how things would work at the weekend, and she wasn't sure if she'd get any time with him at all. After all, Theo usually hung around Wildflower Lock because he was helping her, but now they'd split up, he had his weekends back to do as he pleased.

'You can't blame him,' Bex said. 'This time a week ago, he was messaging Claire and me, buying thousands of fairy lights, and being all excited about the proposal he'd planned. It's been a pretty abrupt turnaround.'

'I suppose,' Daisy responded.

'It's not as if you're happy about things. I think it's safe to say I've never seen you look so miserable.'

'Of course I'm miserable,' Daisy said with a sense of exasperation. 'It's not that I don't love him. I don't get why you guys don't understand that.'

'Oh, we understand it completely,' Bex said, arching an eyebrow. 'It's just that it makes no sense. Despite no evidence at all, you've already predicted the failure of your relationship, which is basically dooming yourself.'

Daisy shook her head. It didn't matter how much she tried to suppress the knots that filled her stomach. Every time she had a minute to think about things, they would return, and conversations like this didn't help. 'You'd understand if you'd been there. It's for the best—'

'In the long run?' Bex interrupted. Her voice was almost a shout. 'I swear, if you're going to say that to me again, I will throw something at you.' She paused, and when she spoke again, her tone was far quieter, though just as harsh. 'And I'm well aware it's not me you're trying to convince when you say that, by the way. You're the one who needs convincing.'

Daisy didn't respond; there wasn't much she could say to that.

Was it the truth? No, she knew she'd made the right decision. She had to have, because if she'd got it wrong... Well, that didn't bear thinking about.

She put down her glass of wine and picked up the remote, ready to change the conversation.

'Okay,' she said. 'I think we're out of new horror movies to watch, which means we're on to thrillers or true crime.'

'Not romance?' Bex said sarcastically.

Daisy shot her a glare. 'True crime it is,' she said, flipping through the channels to find something she wanted to watch. But before she could press play, there was a knock at the door.

'Do you want me to get it?' Bex said, a look of concern on her face.

Daisy shook her head. 'I'll go. It's probably just Francis trying to get me to adopt whatever stray cat she's found this week. Although maybe that's not a bad idea. Maybe I'm destined to become an old cat lady.'

'You'd have to get more than one for that to happen, though,' Bex replied. 'You know that.'

'Well, let's start with one and see how that goes.'

The pair let out a slight chuckle before Daisy walked to the back of the boat and opened the door.

'Hello, love. It's not a bad time, is it?' Her mum was standing on the stern.

Daisy hadn't responded to any of her mother's texts in the past week, or even called to tell her about the situation with Theo, so finding her standing there probably shouldn't have been a surprise. Her mum's normal reaction to Daisy wanting space was to give her anything but. However, what *was* surprising was that her arm was around Nicholas.

'We wanted to know if you and Theo fancied coming to a barbecue on the *Jeanette* this evening.'

Daisy tilted her head to the side, struggling to understand what was going on. Meanwhile, Pippa glanced past Daisy into the boat.

'Hello Bex, dear,' she said. 'I didn't expect to see you here. You're welcome to join us too. The more, the merrier.'

'Right,' Daisy said. 'On the *Jeanette*? With you and Nicholas?'

'Yes, well, given that we're going to be spending a bit more time up north with his family, we thought we should make the most of our days down here. And it's such a lovely one. It seems silly not to have a barbecue, don't you think?'

Daisy was sure she'd slipped into an alternate universe, one where the last four days hadn't happened, one where her mother hadn't turned up on her doorstep and told her that her relationship with Nicholas was over and that Daisy's engagement with Theo was going to end in disaster. Daisy looked to Bex, and the pair exchanged a knowing look that could only be shared between two people who had known each other their entire lives.

'Nicholas?' Bex was suddenly on her feet and moving past Daisy and out onto the stern. 'I wanted to ask you some questions, actually, about sloe gin. I was thinking of making my first batch this year, but I'm not actually sure what sloes are. Any chance there are some here on the canal you could show me?'

Daisy was normally in awe of her friend's spontaneous ability to come up with questions like that, but at that moment, she was too preoccupied, staring at her mother.

'What's going on? You're being very strange about this. I only asked if you wanted to come to a barbecue.'

'You told me things were over between you and Nicholas,' Daisy said. 'You came here, drank my wine, and told me you'd never be getting back together with him.'

A pinkish hue tinted her mother's cheeks as she waved her hand dismissively.

'Oh well, you know what we're like. We bicker, that's all. But you can't believe anything I say after more than a couple of glasses of wine, you know that.'

Daisy could feel her jaw hanging open, the disbelief making it near impossible to speak and yet she forced herself to.

'What about when you said Theo and I shouldn't get married?' she asked. 'What about when you said that I was an idiot for not being able to see that things wouldn't work out? If I had any sense, I'd end things before we got even more embroiled? What about that, Mother? Was I meant to believe you when you said that?'

Pippa's cheeks turned a deep red.

'Daisy, you didn't... I didn't... Oh, darling, please don't tell me that you—' she stammered, unable to finish the sentence.

Daisy finished it for her.

'That I ended things with Theo because of what you said. Yes, Mother. I did. Because I foolishly believed that you were telling me the truth. That you were trying to protect me. That was honestly what I thought you were doing.' It felt as though the world was slipping out beneath her feet, yet somehow she managed to straighten her back. 'Thank you for the barbecue invite,' she said, 'but I think I'll decline. Now, can you please leave?'

76

Daisy didn't know how long she'd been crying, only that she was sure she should've run out of tears by now. But that wasn't the case. From what it appeared, she had an unending supply, although some of them may have been provided by the copious amounts of wine she'd drunk.

'I've really messed this up, really, really messed this up, haven't I?' she said to Bex. What she wanted was for her friend to say it was all okay. To tell her she'd made the right decision and she would see that in the morning, but she didn't.

'Claire is on her way,' Bex said instead. 'You know she's better at giving advice on things like this than I am.'

So there it was – all the confirmation Daisy needed that she had well and truly messed up.

'I should go and speak to him, shouldn't I? I should tell him what happened, what my mum said. I should tell him I was an idiot, and that I don't want anyone else, and I don't – you know, I really don't. Ezra asked for my number at yours, and I said I didn't want to give it to him. All I could think about was how he would never be as perfect as Theo. Why am I such an idiot? Why did I act like this when I know Theo is the one I want to be with?'

'Because you're terrified of relationships and commitment,' Bex said. 'Because you stupidly let your mum amplify those fears and because you were worried he was going to hurt you in the long run, so you wanted to get there first because you—'

'Okay, I didn't need the actual reasons,' Daisy said, fearful of how long the list could go on. 'I need to speak to him. I need to speak to him now.'

The urge to see Theo was greater than any she had ever felt, as if her body were physically being drawn across to the other side of the canal. And yet, as Daisy stood up, Bex followed and placed her hands on Daisy's shoulders.

'I don't think that's the best idea, given the state you're in. Maybe you need to hang on a bit. Wait till tomorrow, wait till you've sobered up.'

'Tomorrow? That means he's going to spend another night thinking I don't want to be with him. I do. I do want to be with him. That's all I want.'

'I get that,' Bex said. 'Maybe just telling him in a more measured manner might be a good idea.' Her hands still hadn't left Daisy's shoulders and when Daisy glanced to the side, she noticed that Bex's wine glass was still full. But just because Bex had drunk a bit less than Daisy, it didn't mean she was right, did it?

Daisy could hear what her friend was saying, but Bex obviously didn't understand. Daisy needed to do this now. She needed to put it right now. She needed to speak to Theo.

'I'm going over there,' she said, already grabbing her bag and heading for the door. 'Tell Claire I won't be long. I love you. Wish me luck.'

'You're sure?' Bex said again, though Daisy responded with just a look. 'Fine, good luck, but I really don't think—'

Whatever else it was she was going to say, Daisy didn't hear. She didn't need to. She was already out of the boat and heading to Theo's.

77

Daisy couldn't remember the towpath being so narrow before, but as she made her way towards Theo, she struggled to stay on the thin strip of tarmac and kept stumbling into the hedgerow. It was probably just the nerves making her dizzy, she reasoned. The nerves and perhaps a little bit of the wine, too. But she would be all right once she was aboard the *Narrow Escape*. She would be fine.

With her hand firmly on the handrail, she crossed over the canal at the lock and promptly hopped onto the *Narrow Escape*.

'Theo! Theo!' She hammered her fist against the door. 'It's me, Theo! I need to speak to you, please.'

She paused, straining to hear if there were any footsteps inside, but all her calls were met with silence. She readied her hand and hammered again.

'Please, Theo, I know I screwed up. I just want to talk to you. Please, please, please listen to me. I've messed up. I can let myself in, you know, I've got a key.' She started to rummage in her bag, only to remember she had given Theo his key back, along with all the belongings she'd packed up.

With a slight sigh, Daisy dropped back, rubbing her head momentarily before straightening up and beginning to knock again.

'I'm not giving up, Theo. I'm not. I won't stop knocking until you let me in. Can you speak to me, please? I need to speak to you.'

Daisy's arm was already aching, and her knuckles were red from constantly rapping against the door, yet she couldn't stop. If she did, he'd think she didn't care, that she gave up too easily. She wasn't going to let that happen. 'I won't give up, Theo, I won't. I'll stay here all night if I have to.'

She paused to catch her breath and was about to start knocking again when a voice spoke to her from behind.

'If you carry on like that, you're going to get a noise complaint, and it's on my boat, so I'd appreciate it if you didn't.'

Theo was standing a short way away, sunglasses on, Johnny's lead held limply at his side as the dog wandered freely towards Daisy.

'Theo, thank God.' Relief billowed through her. 'I'm so sorry. I need to talk to you. I have to talk to you.'

Theo didn't move from where he was standing. 'So I heard. You look like you've had a drink.'

'Please, Theo, I made a mistake. I made a really horrible mistake. I need you to hear me out. I need you to forgive me. Please, Theo.'

She went to approach him, but something about his posture stopped her. His arms were folded across his chest and his back was so straight, it looked rigid.

'I think you need to head back home,' he said. 'You've had far too much to drink.'

'I haven't, I haven't! I mean, I have had a drink, but that doesn't change what I need to say, Theo. Please, if you'd just listen

to me. It wasn't my fault. I was stupid. I listened to my mother,
I—'

'Daisy, please. This is getting ridiculous. Go home. I'm not
doing this.'

'But you will, right? You'll talk to me tomorrow, maybe? Can
we talk tomorrow, please? Please?'

'For crying out loud, Daisy, haven't you already done enough?'

His raised voice stopped her in her tracks, and she looked up
into his eyes as she had thousands of times before, normally just
before he kissed her. But there was no hint of romance or love in
his gaze. Instead, it was a stony glare that fixed down on her.

'I can't keep doing this, Daisy. I can't do it again. I believed you
once. I let myself believe you after all that stuff with Christian—'

'Theo, come on. You know there's never been anybody else
but you. That was a mistake, but it's not like anything happened
this time. I just wasn't sure what I was feeling.'

'I proposed to you. You said yes. You said yes to spending the
rest of your life with me. And then, four days later, you said it was
over. I can't do it, Daisy. I can't do a lifetime of this – a lifetime of
not knowing. Of wondering when you're going to change your
mind again and decide you can't do it. Like it's the toss of a coin.
I'll be living on eggshells my entire life.'

'No, no, you won't be. I promise it wouldn't be like that, Theo.
It's you. It's always been you. You know it has. I just got so over-
whelmed and so confused, and I let everybody get into my head.
Ending things with you was never what I wanted.'

'Really? Because you sure as hell made it sound like you did.'

Daisy was trying to respond. There were so many more things
she needed to say to him, so many things she needed him to hear,
but he just wasn't listening. Why wasn't he listening? She opened
her mouth to try again, only to realise that wasn't the problem.

Theo was listening. He had heard every word she'd said; he just didn't care.

'Go home, Daisy,' Theo said again. 'You've got what you wanted. This is over for good.'

78

Despite the girls' assurances that things would feel better in the morning after some sleep, Daisy soon discovered that wasn't the case.

'He's right to end things. I don't blame him,' Daisy snivelled. On the table beside her, a stack of used, scrunched-up tissues had formed, and she suspected it was going to get a lot higher. Bex was serving at the coffee shop, in between answering her own work emails, and rushing back and forth to check on Daisy. It was the epitome of multitasking. Claire, on the other hand, was the one supplying the words of comfort. Not that they helped. 'It makes sense. I treated him so horribly.'

'No, you didn't,' Claire said. 'You messed up. You did mess up. There's no denying that. But so did he. He made mistakes too, and you forgave him.'

'Yes, but he didn't say he thought it was better not to be with me,' Daisy countered. 'He'd never have said something like that.'

There was no way around it. She had been an idiot. How did she possibly think ending their relationship would make things better in the long run? All that was going to happen was that she would spend her entire life regretting her mistake. She could see it now. The old spinster Daisy, still living in the *September Rose*, hobbling to make cups of coffee, and struggling to carry them in her withered, old hands. And she wouldn't even be able to have cats either. Not if she was going to keep the café open. Health and safety rules wouldn't allow it. Nope. Her future was panned out in front of her. And it was bleak.

'Maybe I should move,' Daisy said. 'I can't stay in Wildflower Lock, not with him so close. But that's the point of a boat, isn't it? I'm meant to be able to set up wherever I want. Maybe I'll put it on the back of a lorry and move to the other side of the country. Stratford-upon-Avon is meant to be lovely. There are lots of boats over there.'

'You're not moving to Stratford-upon-Avon,' Bex said, poking her head into the living room. 'It's way too far for us to travel when you're having one of your breakdowns. You're going to get through this. I promise you are.'

But Daisy didn't want to get through it. What she wanted was to go back to a week ago, when she had known her life was perfect, or as perfect as a life could get, and not felt the need to mess it all up. She wanted to go back to when she had listened to her mother's words of advice, and simply ignore her. What she wanted to do was to take back all the stupid things she had said and done. Yes, there were plenty of things that Daisy wanted to do, but getting over Theo just wasn't one of them.

'Maybe I should try to talk to him,' Daisy said. 'Now that I'm sober. He was angry. And I was drunk. You said that things seem better for people in the morning. Well, maybe that's true for him too. I should ring him, maybe. Yes, that's what I'll do.'

Daisy reached for her phone, only to see the way Claire and Bex exchanged a look.

'What? You think that's the wrong thing to do?'

'I think that's definitely the wrong thing to do,' Bex replied. 'What are you going to do when he doesn't pick up? If you start leaving hundreds of messages and voicemails, that's not exactly going to convince him.'

Daisy could see what she was saying, but it only caused the panic to rise within her.

'But I've got to do something. I've got to let him know I'm serious. That there's nothing more I want than him.'

'Okay, but ringing him isn't the answer,' Claire agreed. 'We already know you tried to call him this morning. At least three times.'

It was true. The first thing Daisy had done when she had woken up was dial Theo's number. She hadn't even checked what time it was. All she knew was that she needed to speak to him. But just like the girls had said, he had ignored it. Given that there was still a fair amount of alcohol in her bloodstream at that time, she had decided that perhaps it was just because it was early and had tried again fifteen minutes later. Then she had wondered if perhaps he had his phone on silent and she just needed to keep trying. Yep. The girls were absolutely right. Ringing him up hadn't worked. And there was no way she was going to knock on his door again. Just thinking about the way he spoke to her was like having daggers piercing her heart. So what other options were there?

She thought about it for a moment before a smile twisted on her lips.

'I know what I'm going to do,' she said. 'But I'm going to need you guys to look after the coffee shop. Is that okay? This might take a bit of time.'

79

It was a two-pronged attack, of which Daisy had thought the first part would take the most time, but once she sat down to do it, everything came naturally. It wasn't her usual style of painting, but then nothing about this situation was normal. Who on earth painted pictures to get their fiancé back? But she needed to use what she was good at, and this was where her skills lay. So with dozens of pieces of postcard-sized paper stacked and ready to be used, she got to work.

The idea came from her trip around London – the visual diary she had made of her journey, using her paintings. The idea was similar, only this time, it was a visual diary of her and Theo's journey together.

The sketches were simple outlines, with just enough detail that you could tell what was going on. The first one was of Theo standing in the shadow in the *Narrow Escape*, followed by one of the pair of them standing on the towpath with hands raised in what was clearly an argument. But that was where the rows ended. Next came their first trip to the boatyard, followed by their first kiss. Then came Daisy's trip in Slimbridge, with Johnny in between them. There were so many memories she wanted to put down on paper that she could have easily spent weeks doing them all, but time was paramount and so she had to be selective. Amongst the memories she chose was the time Daisy decided she wanted to fly a kite for the first time, and so Theo took her to a kite festival. There was the day when they went to Hever Castle in Kent and the entire field was covered in bluebells and one in Heybridge, where they would frequently drive the boat too. And then, at some point, she reached the more recent paintings. The ones that were going to make her heart ache.

'Okay, we are all cleared up for the day,' Bex said. 'I'm going to have to get off. Are you okay? Claire says she can stay with you tonight.'

Daisy looked up from the painting she was working on, only to find her neck muscles had seized. She had no idea how long she had been in the same position, moving from one picture to the next and back again each time a layer had dried, but it was long enough for her body to feel the effects. Still, she was about to carry on anyway when a sudden thought struck.

'Crap, I'm meant to walk Johnny. I can't see Theo, though. Not yet, not now,' she said, looking at Claire pleadingly. 'I don't suppose you could get him, could you? And maybe walk him? I just really want to get this done.'

'You don't want to see Johnny?' Claire said, sounding nearly as concerned about this comment as she had about the actual breakup.

'Of course I want to see him. But I'll be able to see him a lot more if I patch things up with Theo, and I really need to get this done. Please?'

'Sure.' Claire nodded, though the look of concern remained on her face. 'Yes, I'll go and get him now.'

'Thank you.' Daisy offered her a fleeting smile before turning to Bex. 'And I don't suppose you can do me a favour before you go too, can you?'

Bex looked at her, but unlike Claire, her immediate response wasn't to smile and agree. Instead, her eyes narrowed on Daisy.

'Why do I get the feeling that I'm not going to like this?'

'You are,' Daisy said. 'I promise. I just need you to find a place for me. Well, two places, actually.'

80

The light had faded by the time Daisy finished her paintings. The last ones had definitely been the toughest, both technically and emotionally. Getting the *September Rose* to sparkle with all the fairy lights was a hard thing to pull off in watercolours, and she wasn't entirely sure she had achieved it. She would have certainly been able to do a better job with more time, or if she had managed to go five minutes without crying. But it was hard. Drawing Theo on one knee, there in front of Daisy as she covered her mouth with her hand in surprise, was enough to make her tear up each time she tried to finish it. Out of all the paintings, that one had definitely been the hardest so far, although the future ones – the ones she wanted him to see the most – were even tougher.

She drew the pair of them under an archway, her in a white dress and him in a suit, Johnny beside them with a bow tie in place of his collar. After that, she drew herself pushing a pram. It wasn't meant to please him; she realised that now. She wanted everything life had to offer with Theo, and that included children. Or maybe just a child. It was only the realisation that she might not have them with him that had made her understand how much she truly wanted it. The future pictures didn't stop there, though. The last one she painted they had grey hair and walking sticks, and although Daisy knew that it was impossible, she still had Johnny in the pictures, only this time he was being fussed over by young children.

When they were all done, she sat back in her seat, only to realise something was wrong. Claire wasn't back yet.

No sooner had she thought that than Claire walked in after a ridiculously long walk – over two hours, in fact.

'Where did you go?' Daisy asked. 'I was expecting you ages ago.'

'Yeah.' A flash of guilt crossed Claire's face. 'When I got to the *Escape*, Theo said that he'd been cooped up most of the day and needed a decent walk, so I took him up to the pub that we went to when... when...'

Daisy didn't need her to finish the sentence.

'It's okay. Honestly. Come and have a look. Tell me what you think of these.'

After washing her hands and taking off her shoes, Claire moved over to the table, where she leaned over Daisy's shoulder to look at the paintings.

'Daisy, these are incredible. They really are. He will see them. He'll understand. I'm sure of it.'

It was exactly what Daisy needed to hear. She just hoped Claire wasn't saying it simply to please her.

'Well, I'm not finished yet,' she said. 'I still need to write a letter.'

'A letter?'

Daisy nodded. 'Maybe he won't listen to me when I speak, but hopefully, when he reads what I've written, he'll know I'm telling the truth. If he gives me another chance, then I'll never mess it up again.'

81

Dear Theo

I have lost count of how many attempts I have taken to try to get this letter right, but I've realised that maybe that's the whole point. I won't be able to. I will never be able to get everything right, and I will never be able to make up for the hurt that I've caused you. I know that. But I want one last chance to try. Please, I know that you're entirely within your right to crumple up this paper and never offer it a second glance, but if you would just do me one last thing and read through this in its entirety, it will be the last thing I ever ask of you. After this, it is up to you. If you decide that this is over for good, then I will respect that. I won't pester you. I won't intrude on your life. But I just want this one last time to say I'm sorry, I'm an idiot. You are the love of my life and I would do anything to repair the mess I've made.

It's wrong to blame other people for my actions these last few days. And I'm not going to do that. I said the words I said to you. I am responsible for what I did, but I still want you to know why. And that's because I believe, or rather I did believe, that I was never really deserving of your love. And that is my failing, not yours.

I let other people's opinions affect my thoughts. I believed my mother's drunken words. I believed your parents' disparaging comments. But worse than that, I believed my own insecurities. And I wish to God I hadn't. I love you, Theo. I love you with all my heart.

Whatever happens, I know now that my future is meant to be with you, because you bring out the best in me. And, as arrogant as it sounds, I believe I bring out the best in you, too. I laugh with you like I laugh with no one else. I take risks with you that I would never consider with anyone else. You make me feel safe. You make me feel invincible. You are everything.

And I get why you are afraid that I will do this again. I understand why you would think that sometime in the future, I will panic and get scared and decide to run again, but I won't. I know for certain that I won't. I have felt this loss, Theo. I have felt the way my heart is breaking so intensely in my chest that I can't breathe, and I will never do it again. I know you have to trust me to believe that, but please, I swear on my life, yours, and that of our future family…

I can't say I know exactly what I want in the way of 2.4 children, like some people do. But I can say that when I think of us in old age, I imagine us cooking up big family feasts, with children running around our ankles. I imagine Christmas mornings where presents are piled high beneath the tree and children are tearing hastily at the wrapping, and Christmas dinners where we open our crackers and place party hats on our heads to eat the massive feast that we have prepared together.

I imagine holidays, not just local ones in the boats, but ones far further afield, where we see the world together. And these things I see, Theo, they are so clear in my mind. So vivid,

I can't for one minute believe they are just a figment of my imagination. They are the future. The future I want. And the future I believe we can make happen.

You may think I'm being overly sentimental or dramatic as you read this, but it's true. I never thought that I would find someone as kind and fun and generous as you. Someone as supportive and hardworking who always lifts me up every time I'm down and never makes me feel ridiculous, even when I do ridiculous things, like adopting a random stray dog. You are everything I could have dreamed of, and I just didn't believe that dreams could last. At some point, I assumed I would have to wake up.

I think that's why things became harder after the proposal. Because of things your parents said, and mine, I began to believe that sooner or later, you were going to realise the truth. You were going to realise that I wasn't good enough for you and you were going to want better. And I'm not shifting the blame to you in any way, but I think partly the ring confirmed that for me. Someday, I believed you would wake up and realise that there was a girl out there who was deserving of her own ring.

I'm not saying these thoughts are rational or reasonable. I'm just trying to let you know why I did what I did. That's why I got there first. That's why I thought that by ending things the way I did, I was saving us both from heartache. Now, of course, I realise what a mistake I've made, in that I've quite possibly robbed myself of the best future I could have had. And... I think... robbed you of it, too. Because as strange as it sounds, these last few days without you have shown me that I really am deserving of true love.

My friends are the thing that has proved this to me. I don't

*think you can get friends as good without being someone
people can truly rely on.*

*I know I'm deserving of love. I see that now. But I also see
that the only person I want to share that love with is you. And
so, here is my last attempt. If you feel the same as me, and
God, I hope that you do, then please meet me at 22 Chester
Road, Sunday at 11 a.m. It should all make sense then.*

I hope to see you there.

Yours always, whatever happens,

Daisy

82

Daisy felt sick with nerves. Her stomach had twisted itself into so many knots that she could barely sip at the glass of water in front of her. And all she could do was wait.

'So, do you want to get started now? I can run through it all with you now and then with your friend when they come if you want? Maybe you could look—'

'No,' Daisy cut across the woman before she could say any more. 'We'll wait until he gets here.'

'Okay.' The woman brushed her hands on her apron before moving over to the other side of the studio.

Daisy checked her watch. Why had she come early? Parking was one of the reasons. She knew that spaces around the studio were limited and she hadn't wanted to drive up and down the roads, stressing that she wouldn't find a place and worrying that she was going to be late. But it had been surprisingly easy to find somewhere for the car, and now she was here with all this time to wait. She had told Theo explicitly to come at eleven, and yet Daisy had been there since twenty to, her pulse racing with every passing minute. She had not had the courage to give him the paintings and letter directly, but instead had placed them on the stern of his boat, meaning that all she could do was assume he had seen them. That he had looked at the paintings and read the letter properly. There was a chance, of course, that he had just picked up the entire package and thrown it straight into the canal. That thought was enough to make the nerves billow through her at unprecedented speed, but she couldn't dwell on them. Besides, that didn't seem like a very Theo thing to do.

Daisy looked at the clock on the wall and compared it to the one on her phone and the watch on her wrist. They all said exactly the same time. Two minutes to eleven. Theo would be here. He would. She just had to wait.

A message pinged on her phone, causing her stomach to somersault, although when she looked down it was Claire wishing her good luck.

We are here if you need us, the message read.

Did she know something? Daisy panicked. Did she know that Theo wasn't coming, and that was why she had reminded her they were there if she needed help? Maybe it was. She picked up her phone, ready to ring Claire and check, only to change her mind. She wasn't going to jump to conclusions. Not until she knew for sure. That was what she tried to tell herself, although her mind was already racing. No matter how much she had tried to work through the worst-case scenario of Theo not coming, she hadn't wanted to believe it. She had been so convinced that this would work. That the letter and the paintings would work and once he was here, she would show him it was forever. But as she looked up at the clock again, it was as if her entire world had dropped away. It was 11.01. Theo was never late. He was probably the most punctual person Daisy had ever known. And for important events, he was always early. Always. Only he wasn't there. Which meant only one thing. He wasn't coming.

Daisy tried to stand up, only her legs didn't want to move. Her head was spinning, and she could feel her body rocking back and forth as she tried to balance.

'Is everything okay?' the woman said, moving across to her. 'You look a little peaky.'

'I'm really sorry, I can't... I don't think... I'm sorry.' She could barely see for the tears that were blurring her eyes. 'I'll send you the money. I'm sorry... I just can't.'

She stumbled backwards, her eyes still on the clock, praying there had been a mistake, but there wasn't. Two minutes past. Theo wasn't coming.

As she bent over and grabbed her bag from the ground, she stumbled backwards, eyes down, not even noticing as the door swung open.

'Sorry,' Daisy said as she moved to go, only to see her way was blocked.

'Don't tell me you're leaving already?'

She lifted her gaze, not wanting to believe the voice that rang around in her head. Blinking, she drew in a breath, only for the tears to tumble faster than ever. It was Theo. Theo was there, and he was looking straight down at her. But he hadn't come on time. What did that mean?

'Parking in this place is a nightmare,' he said.

'It is.' Her words came out in a half cough as she struggled to smile, but she couldn't manage it. 'I didn't think you were going to come,' she said. 'I thought... I thought...'

'I'm here, Daisy. And I'm not going anywhere.'

She nodded. All she wanted to do was kiss him. She needed to kiss him, and yet she couldn't. She wouldn't believe it was real, not unless he kissed her first. No sooner had the thought entered her head than Theo leaned forward.

'No more running away scared?' he whispered.

'Never.'

Daisy wasn't sure how long the kiss lasted. It could only have been a few seconds at most, and yet it was undoubtedly the most important kiss of her life. In that single moment, it felt like everything in her world had fallen back into place.

'Excuse me? Are you ready to begin? I just want to give you as much time as possible. I'm assuming neither of you have designed your own jewellery before?'

It was then that Daisy finally managed to show the smile that had been filling her heart since Theo entered the studio, even though her eyes were still filled with tears.

'No,' she said. 'We haven't.'

'Great, well, let's talk through some ideas. What is it you are hoping to make, exactly?'

Daisy looked at Theo. She hadn't mentioned this to him, and for a split second feared she had made a bad call, but when she saw the grin on his face, she knew she had picked the right place to show him how committed she was.

'An engagement ring,' Theo said to the jeweller, though he was still looking at Daisy as he spoke. 'We want to design an engagement ring.'

EPILOGUE

Daisy and Theo came up with the design together. One large rectangular sapphire – or baguette, as the jeweller called the shape – with two smaller emeralds of the same shape on either side. The lock and the two sides of the towpath. It was the place that had brought them together, and now it would be with Daisy wherever she went. There on her ring finger. It was two weeks before they could pick it up and only another two weeks before it was joined with a simple silver band.

'You sure?' Theo said, as they stood outside the registry office. 'This is definitely what you want?'

'This is absolutely what I want,' Daisy said. 'No fuss, no expenses – just us promising to spend the rest of our lives with one another.'

'Then there's no way I can say no to that.' Theo grinned back.

There was probably going to be some fallout from the way they were doing things. Daisy knew that, but she didn't care. She wasn't getting married to make other people happy. She didn't need to fit whatever conventions they wanted to place on her.

This was what she wanted. Theo. Pure and simple. She moved forward to kiss him, only for a bark to interrupt her.

'Yes, I know. Don't worry, you're coming in there with us,' she said, reaching down to straighten Johnny's bow tie, only for Bex to stop her.

'I'll do that. You don't want dog fur all over you before the event,' she said, then promptly adjusted the bow tie.

Bex, Claire and Johnny. That was it. They were all the people who were going to be present for the wedding. Daisy knew Amelia had wanted to come too, but it was only two witnesses that they needed, and she wanted the whole thing to be as simple as it could be. And that meant having the two friends who had been by her side through it all standing there with her.

They had discussed having a party at some point. Maybe a nice meal out with family, or at the Lock so that their friends there got to celebrate too, but that was all secondary to Daisy. What mattered was her and Theo. He made her the best version of herself, just like she did with him. They were a partnership. A couple who found joy in each other's happiness. And that day, the wedding day, was just the beginning of the rest of their lives together.

* * *

MORE FROM HANNAH LYNN

Another book from Hannah Lynn, *In at the Deep End*, is available to order now here:

www.mybook.to/InattheDeepEndBackAd

ACKNOWLEDGEMENTS

My first acknowledgement has to go to you, my readers. I hope you have enjoyed this final trip to Wildflower Lock and the conclusion of Daisy and Theo's relationship. I have absolutely adored writing this series of books. It has been pure escapism for me, and I hope for you all too. You are the reason I am lucky enough to have this incredible career, I am grateful for each and every person's support.

There are, of course, a few more thanks I need to give.

To my editor, Emily, who is always so supportive as well as hugely skilled. Thank you for helping this series be the best it could possibly be, and to the rest of the Boldwood team for all they do.

To the dozens of people who I have sought help from during this series, from friends, like Kate, and Kelly, whose boat knowledge has been indispensable, to the staff at Essex Waterways, Papermill Lock, and all the various boat yards I have rung! I have only ever been offered advice and support and I am so grateful for that.

Lastly to Jake. You are the best partner in life I could wish for, although I was hoping that writing this series would convince you that we needed to move onto a narrowboat and you're still not fully onboard yet. (Did you like the pun?!) Still, I did have some lovely trips on them under the guise of research! Thank you for being such a great captain.

ABOUT THE AUTHOR

Hannah Lynn is the author of over twenty books spanning several genres. Hannah grew up in the Cotswolds, UK. After graduating from university, she spent 15 years as a teacher of physics, teaching in the UK, Thailand, Malaysia, Austria and Jordan.

Sign up to Hannah Lynn's mailing list here for news, competitions and updates on future books.

Visit Hannah's website: www.hannahlynnauthor.com

Follow Hannah on social media:

facebook.com/hannahlynnauthor

instagram.com/hannahlynnwrites

bookbub.com/authors/hannah-lynn

Boldwood

Boldwood Books is an award-winning fiction publishing company seeking out the best stories from around the world.

Find out more at www.boldwoodbooks.com

Join our reader community for brilliant books, competitions and offers!

Follow us
@BoldwoodBooks
@TheBoldBookClub

Sign up to our weekly deals newsletter

https://bit.ly/BoldwoodBNewsletter